LEAVE DEAD ENOUGH ALONE

A SAM LAWSON MYSTERY BOOK 8

DAVID K. WILSON

1

IT WAS night at the Burdett County Courthouse and Amy Booker was the only person left in the small, two-story building. Truth be told, she was probably the only person left in the entire downtown area of Burdett, Texas. With a population of just over 1,000 people, there wasn't much demand for anything to stay open much past five. Leave that to the late-night fast-food restaurants up near the state highway.

But here, in the small County Clerk's office of the small courthouse in one of the smallest counties in East Texas, Amy sat on the floor, sifting through a pile of documents. She blew a wisp of blonde hair away from her eyes as she furiously scribbled names and numbers into her notebook. Turning to the next document, she paused to push her large red glass frames up the bridge of her nose. Glancing up at the clock, she was surprised to see it was already nine o'clock.

Have I really been doing this for three hours? she wondered.

She bit her lower lip as she skimmed the document, swearing it would be the last for the night. She found the information she needed, then copied it into her notebook.

"Okay. That's enough," she said out loud.

She shut her notebook and put the documents back in their proper file folders and the file folders back in the proper file cabinets. The sound of the file drawer slamming shut echoed through the empty building. Then she gathered her things and tossed them both in her oversized purse, slipped on her shoes, flipped off the lights, and shut the County Clerk's office door behind her. She only lived fifteen minutes away, in the neighboring town of Elsip, so she could easily be home by 9:30. Even though her husband was unemployed, he was probably still out enjoying some after work drinks. That meant she would have some nice alone time for a bath and a good cozy mystery.

Other than an occasional domestic disturbance, Burdett hadn't seen any violent crimes for years. It was probably about as safe as any city could be after dark. Still, Amy had seen enough true crime movies to still be nervous as she walked through the empty building.

She picked up her pace, her eyes glued on the main doors of the building, which stood about thirty yards in front of her. On the other side, everything was pitch black.

They still haven't fixed the parking lot light, she griped to herself.

She had complained several times to both her boss and the building supervisor, although some would argue her meek, quiet tone was more of a polite suggestion rather than a stern complaint.

Amy had always been soft-spoken and reserved. Ten years out of high school, she was still known as the Library Girl, a moniker gifted to her by fellow classmates. Her life over the past decade had only reinforced the nickname. As the index clerk for Burdett County, she happily spent most of her days filing and maintaining all kinds of public records. In a world that had gone mainly digital, she had one of the few jobs left that still dealt with actual paper documents. She was a pretty woman but had always felt self-conscious about her looks. She hid behind large glasses, frizzy blonde hair and baggy clothes that all seemed a couple of sizes two large.

Gus Booker, her husband of just over ten years, had always been frustrated with the way Amy hid her beauty. But try as he might to get her to change — which really amounted to nothing more than him complaining — she stayed securely hidden inside herself.

That was one of the many wedges that had come between the couple. These days, they barely tolerated each other's company. Silence had become their shared language, and they avoided each other as much as possible. It's why Gus spent most of his time at a local bar, and why she stayed late at the County Clerk's Office, indulging her hobby of building a record of her hometown's history. A hobby that had recently led her to an accidental discovery. She needed to do a little bit more cross-checking before she brought it up to her boss, but she may have stumbled upon something very interesting. And possibly criminal.

Amy locked the bolt on the main doors of the courthouse, took a deep breath, and walked quickly to her car, which sat alone in the middle of the dark parking lot. Once again, the town's actual low crime rate contradicted the conditioning of just about anything she'd ever seen or read. The rule was simple: Lone women should avoid dark parking lots at all costs. Nothing good could ever come from it.

When Amy saw the headlights of an approaching car slice through the darkness, she was half relieved that she was no longer alone. But when the car pulled up right next to her own, Amy's heart sped up as her pace slowed down. The car's headlights shown in her face and she raised her hand to block the brightness. She hadn't been able to get a good look at the car, and now she couldn't see it at all.

Amy swallowed her fear and told herself that there was nothing to be afraid of. It was a small town, and she was almost guaranteed to know who was waiting for her. She started walking to her car again, her breath caught in her throat.

Just as she reached her car, she heard the door to the mystery car open behind her and then a voice.

"Amy."

Amy spun around and almost collapsed in relief.

"Oh, my goodness," she said, out of breath. "You scared me to death."

Amy watched, confused, as the familiar face walked around the car and opened the passenger door.

"Get in."

The stern look let her instantly know something was wrong.

"I... I really need to get going," Amy stammered.

The reply was serious. Even threatening. "Get in. Now."

2

———————

Sam stood in the bed of his black F-150 pickup, securing the last of his camping gear with a bungee cord. He looked down at his secured masterpiece, a jumbled web of elastic bungee cords stretched over haphazard piles of camping and fishing gear.

"There," he said proudly, oblivious to the disorganized mess he had created.

He hopped out of the truck bed, ignoring the shot of pain that ran through his knee as he hit the driveway's pavement. Even though Sam was by no means in bad shape for a man in his late-40s, he carried enough scars and bruises to make any physical activity a cry for help.

He triumphantly slid in one final item, his prized tackle box, before shutting the tailgate.

"All set and ready to go," he announced to his wife. "And it's barely 7 o'clock."

Carla had been watching her husband pack up his truck for a weekend fishing trip with his old cop buddies. It had been a while since Sam had been a detective with the Quinton Police Department, and he had jumped at the chance to spend a weekend with his old friends.

Sam slid his hands around his wife's waist and pulled her to him.

Not a day went by that Sam didn't wonder how a smart, gorgeous, amazing woman like Carla had decided to marry a man like him. Tall, lean and beautiful, she looked like she could be walking a runway in Milan instead of poking dead people at the county morgue. But as the chief medical examiner for Hubbard County, she was revered all over Texas as one of the best in the state.

"She's the perfect woman," Sam would often joke. "Smart, beautiful, and terrible taste in men."

"You sure you're going to be okay without me?" Sam teased.

"I will find a way to manage on my own," Carla replied with a wink. "You just enjoy yourself. Within reason."

"I will do my best," Sam said. "But I make no promises."

Carla's cell phone rang and, as she stepped away to answer it, Sam turned to his truck, performing a mental checklist of supplies for the umpteenth time.

"Sam," Carla said.

He had heard that tone before. It was never followed by anything Sam wanted to hear. He let out a groan and slowly turned to see Carla holding the phone against her chest.

"I think you should take this," she half-whispered.

"Oh, no, no, no, no. I am on vacation," he replied, shaking a finger at her. "No new cases. Tell them it will have to wait until I get back."

"I don't think this can," Carla said, an apologetic look on her face.

Sam shut his eyes, quietly saying goodbye to his fishing trip, then took the phone from her.

A two-hour drive later, Judy Duncan sat across from Sam in their living room, blowing into a tissue that Carla had just handed her. She was a thin, pale woman, probably in her early thirties. Sam could tell every muscle in her body was clenched tight in worry. Her shoulders were bunched up high and one of her knees bounced nervously.

"You don't understand. It's just not like her," Judy

said. "She wouldn't just take off like this. And no one is taking me seriously."

Judy pulled off her thick glasses to wipe the tears from her bloodshot eyes.

"Did you talk to law enforcement?" Sam asked gently.

"Of course. But the sheriff won't take me seriously. Said it happens all the time and to just go home and wait. And my good-for-nothing brother-in-law is convinced she left him for some other guy."

"You think that's possible?" Carla asked.

Judy shook her head. "No! Not that I wouldn't blame her. But that's just not who she is. I know my sister. This isn't like her! It's been four days! The sheriff won't even issue a missing persons report. That's why I drove all the way up here this morning. I hardly ever leave my house, but I just need someone to believe me!"

She began to cry again, and Carla moved next to her on the couch to console her. She also shot Sam a look that spoke a thousand words. Sam knew he didn't have much of a choice.

"It's not that I don't believe you, ma'am," Sam said. "It's just that—"

Carla's scolding glare cut the words short and Sam quickly backtracked.

"It's just that I need to remain objective. Consider all angles. It's how the P.I. mind works."

Judy looked up, choking back her sobs.

"Does that mean you'll find her?"

Sam exhaled slowly, giving in to his conscience – and Carla's pleading stare.

"Where did you say she lived again?" he asked.

"Burdett County," Judy answered, hope in her voice. "Elsip."

Sam thought about it.

"I suppose that's not too far out of my way," he thought out loud. "I could swing by on my way to the lake. Talk to a few people. Do a little digging."

Judy nodded excitedly. "Thank you so much!"

"But you have to be prepared for me to tell you the same thing the sheriff did," Sam said. "I've dealt with cases like this a thousand times and nine times out of ten, the missing person shows back up without incident. Just a lot of apologies."

Judy stood and hugged Carla. She rushed to Sam and hugged him also.

"I hope you're right," she said. "I already feel better knowing you'll look into it."

Sam smiled half-heartedly. Hopefully, it would be as cut and dried as he said, and he could still meet up with his friends by nightfall. He'd miss a day of fishing, but he'd make some easy money and Judy could get a little peace of mind. A win-win for everyone.

Still, Sam knew better than to get his hopes up too

much about a missing persons case, regardless of what he had said to Judy. If Amy Booker was the type of person her sister had described, it was less likely she just took off without telling anyone. Her sister had every reason to be concerned.

3

____

Sam hit the road pretty much right after Judy left. He figured there was no sense wasting the daylight. This way, he'd have plenty of time to ask around about Amy and still make it to the lake before it got too late. Nights around the campfire were the best part of these trips. Trading tall tales and dirty jokes, the kind that got a little longer and a little filthier every year. It was an antidote for pretty much any kind of stress. In fact, the nights were so fun, spending the day on the lake fishing was really just a way to pass the time until the next night.

Sam drove past the small green sign announcing his arrival to Elsip, Population 125. If it wasn't for the sign, Sam would have had no idea he had arrived. There was no real town to speak of. No buildings. No schools. Just lots of trees and small asphalt roads veering off the state highway. Sam had seen dozens of these small, unincorporated communities made up of nothing more than a sprinkling of homes and trailer parks. Typically, the people mostly worked at a nearby factory of some sort. From the dank odor in the air, Sam figured there had to be a poultry factory nearby. Most days, the smell would diffuse in the breeze and was barely noticeable. But on a hot, still, humid day like this one, the stench would hang low, like week old trash that had been sitting out in the hot sun. It was the kind of smell that would crawl into your clothes and come home with you. From the smell of things, Sam was surprised that 125 people still lived in town.

Sam checked his GPS. He was only a few minutes away from his first stop: the home of Amy and Gus Booker. His computerized navigator led him through a maze of backroads that finally brought him to a small collection of houses clustered together in the middle of nowhere. He pulled into the gravel driveway of an old ranch house. It looked worn and tired, like it had given up years ago. The maroon paint was chipped and fading, and the chain link fence that surrounded a portion of the front yard was leaning so badly, Sam worried it would topple at the slightest touch.

Before he could get out of his truck, the screen door on the side of the house squeaked open. A tall man with no shirt, greasy brown hair and two-day stubble stumbled out. Sam had already gotten the rundown on Gus Booker from Judy, keeping in mind that a suspicious sister-in-law was not likely to paint the most flattering picture. But in this case, she was spot on. Gus had the neglected body of an ex-athlete who had traded his love of the game for a six-pack-a-night habit. But he walked with the confidence and swagger of someone who still saw himself as that high school quarterback who all the girls adored. Talk about conditioned confidence. A beautiful woman will look in a mirror and see flaws that don't even exist. A man that has no business taking his shirt off will look in that same mirror and see a work of art.

"Who are you?" Gus asked.

Oh, good, thought Sam. *No small talk. That'll save me time.*

"Mr. Booker?" Sam said as professionally as he could, given his present company. "I'm a private investigator looking into your wife's disappearance."

A big grin broke across Gus's face, and he let out a laugh that sounded like a wounded cat.

"That damn Judy put you up to this, didn't she?" he asked.

"She's a little concerned," Sam answered.

"Well, good on you making some easy money," Gus continued, ignoring Sam. "Cuz there ain't nothing to look in to. I know exactly where she is."

Sam was surprised by that response.

"You do? Did she come home?"

"Hell, naw," Gus said. "That bitch done run off with Jason Mackey."

"Who's Jason Mackey?" Sam asked, scrambling for his notepad.

"He's a backstabbing dirtbag who's as good as dead next time I see him."

"And you're sure she ran off with him?" Sam asked.

Gus reached on top of the old refrigerator that sat under the carport next to the side door and pulled down a pack of Marlboros. He popped a cigarette into his mouth, pulled a lighter from his jeans pocket and took a long drag, never taking his eyes off of Sam.

"Well, she didn't run off, per se," Gus finally said, his body swaying back and forth as if he was standing on a boat. "But I bet he's got her all shacked up at his place. You go check it out. I guarantee you'll find that little bitch hiding in his bedroom. And you can tell her she can stay there, for all I care."

Sam wrote down Jason Mackey's name but had a strong feeling that would lead to a dead-end. It's hard to hide out in a small town, no matter how far apart the houses are. Still, if Amy was having an affair, it could be a lead he'd need to check into. If he was lucky, Gus would be right, and Sam could be on his way.

But while he was at the Booker's house, he needed to take a look around inside. He knew Gus wasn't just going to let him in his house to snoop around, so he decided to take a few liberties with his reasons.

"Do you mind if I look around inside your house anyways?" Sam said. "Just so I earn my money?"

Gus took another long drag from his cigarette and blew the smoke out slowly. He grinned.

"Well, you got me in a tight spot there, hombre," Gus said. "If I refuse, I'm going to look uncooperative. Like I'm hiding something. But if I let you in, you're gonna start going through my shit. And I don't like the sound of that."

"Believe me," Sam said. "I don't like the sound of that either. I'll be go through as little shit as possible. I promise."

"What do you think you're going to find?"

Sam shrugged. "Probably nothing. But we could find out if she stole anything from you."

Sam watched Gus think it over. He hoped that appealing to Gus's paranoia would do the trick. And it seemed to be doing just that. Gus started nodding his head.

"That's a damn good idea," Gus said. "If I say she

stole something, people'll think I'm lying. But if you say it, they'll have to believe me."

Gus opened the door and held it for Sam.

"Hurry up," he said. "You're letting all the flies in."

From the look of things, the flies had already taken up residence and signed a long-term lease.

4

—————

SAM FOLLOWED the flies into the disaster zone that had once been a kitchen. Dishes, pots and pans were stacked in the sink and all over the counter. Scraps of food sat half eaten on the counters and small round kitchen table.

"Amy did most of the cleaning around here," Gus said, stepping over a pizza box and walking into a dark living room. Sam looked around in disbelief. Amy had only been gone a couple of days at this point.

How could he have done that much damage in such a short amount of time?

The living room only fared a little better. Half-crushed beer cans littered the orange shag carpet and dark green couch. Gus plopped down in a tattered leather recliner held together by duct tape and wishful thinking. He plopped out the footrest, pulled a bottle of beer from a mini-cooler stationed to his side and popped the top with a pocketknife. He held it up to Sam.

"Cold one?" he asked.

Sam shook his head as he took in his surroundings. Aside from the bottles and cans, the room was pretty sparse. A large flat-screen TV sat on a stack of cinder blocks directly in front of Gus. A tapestry behind the couch bore the image of two wolves howling at a full moon. A ten-point buck hung from one of the dark paneled walls. A handmade bookshelf, put together from a series of two by fours sitting across even more cinder blocks, covered the far wall. It was lined with books and a few trophies. As Gus turned on a daytime game show, Sam walked across the room to get a better look at the bookcase. The trophies were what he expected. High school trophies. Football championships. Track. A baseball MVP award.

"Quite the athlete," Sam said out loud.

"You know it," Gus said. "Most of my records still stand to this day."

"Really?" Sam feigned interest. There were few things more annoying to him than adults still bragging about their high school athletic achievements. To be fair, this was probably because Sam didn't have much to brag about in that department. He had played football.

He grew up in Texas. It was practically a birthright. But he was like most other kids playing sports — average at best.

"I shit you not," Gus replied. "There was even talk of renaming the high school stadium after me at some point."

"Impressive," Sam said, not believing Gus for a second.

He scanned the books. Clearly, these were the part of the shelf that belonged to Amy. Her taste ran the full gamut. From cheap romance novels to books by authors that Sam recognized: Jane Austen, John Steinbeck, Virginia Woolf and Agatha Christie. Lots of Agatha Christie books. And tons of mystery books.

"If Amy took any of those books, she can have 'em," Gus said. "But if she touched any of the DVDs on the bottom shelf, those are mine."

Sam nodded and pointed at an open door next to the bookshelf. "What's in here?"

"That's the boo-door," Gus said, trying to sound fancy but mispronouncing boudoir badly. "Light switch is to your right. Just don't go through any of the drawers. That's private."

The bedroom was about as messy as the rest of the house. It was small and didn't consist of much more than a full-size mattress that lay on the floor, sheets tossed and turned and spread all over. From the half-eaten slice of pizza on a pillow, it was clear that Gus had no problem with eating in bed. Once again, Gus had managed to create more of a mess in two days than most men could do in a month. Sam was almost impressed. A small dresser sat against one wall. The top was littered with beer cans, an ash tray and a football propped on a kicking tee. Once again, nothing about Amy seemed to exist anywhere.

"Have you done any cleaning since Amy left?" Sam yelled into the living room.

"No way," Gus yelled back. "I'm saving it all for that bitch when she comes crawling back. I'll let her stay long enough to clean this all up, then I'll kick her out for good."

Amy was invisible in her own house, Sam thought. *I wouldn't blame her a bit if she took off.*

He poked around a bit more but knew he wasn't going to find anything that would lead him to Amy's whereabouts. And he had a few more people to talk to before he could report back to Judy and claim he did his due diligence. He said his goodbyes to Gus and gave him his card, making him promise to call if Amy showed up again.

"When she shows up," Gus corrected Sam. "It's not if, it's when. You wait and see. I know my Amy."

Sam nodded with a smirk. He was willing to bet Gus didn't know a single thing about his wife and didn't care to, either. Sam couldn't help but hope Amy had run off. Hopefully, she wouldn't want to return to this. But he reminded himself that he was getting paid to find her. And that meant he next needed to pay a visit to the man Gus had accused of having an affair with Amy: Jason Mackey.

5

ACCORDING TO GUS, Jason Mackey lived just outside of town right off the state highway. Sam had begun to slow down to try and spot mile marker 72, which was right before the turn-off to Jason's house. But no sooner than he'd started looking, he noticed a brown and white SUV coming up behind him. An SUV with lights on the roof. It was a Sheriff's vehicle.

The lights flashed off and on, in sync with a few blips on the siren. Sam pulled over on the shoulder, getting his ID, registration, gun permit and Private Investigator badge ready. He looked in his rear-view mirror as a tall, lanky man stepped out of the vehicle. He was slightly bow-legged, which gave him a cocky walk like an old cowboy. As he sauntered toward Sam's truck, he straightened his tan cowboy hat with one hand and smoothed his thick, white mustache with the other. He knelt at Sam's window, looking at Sam with friendly, green eyes.

"Howdy there," he said in a soft baritone voice as smooth as butter. "You know what I pulled you over for?"

His eyes scanned the cab of Sam's truck, taking in every detail. His skin was tan and weathered, and his face was lined with wrinkles from squinting into the sun. Sam figured him to be in his late 60s, give or take a decade.

"I didn't think I was speeding," Sam said.

He held out his license and registration for the sheriff, but the lawman didn't seem too interested.

"You were out at Gus Booker's place," he said.

News sure travels fast in a small town, Sam thought.

"Yes, sir," Sam said. "I'm a private investigator looking into the disappearance of his wife, Amy."

Sam showed his P.I. badge to the sheriff. Again, the sheriff didn't seem that interested. Instead, he grinned and gave a slow, neutral "mmhmm". Sam couldn't tell if it was a polite acknowledgement or if the sheriff was filing away information for later.

"And that's why I stopped you," the sheriff said. "I'm Sheriff Wheeler. I imagine you were coming to see me at some point. Why don't you follow me in? It's only about ten minutes up the road."

Without waiting for an answer, Sheriff Wheeler leaned up, patted Sam's truck door and walked back to his car.

Sam followed the sheriff into Burdett. While much more of a town than Elsip, it still consisted of little more than a cluster of buildings surrounding a small, town square park. Sam couldn't help but notice that, out of the dozen buildings butted up against each other, two of them were churches: The First Baptist Church and Faith Baptist Church. The sheriff's SUV turned right at the stop sign and into the parking lot behind the Burdett County Courthouse. While the sheriff pulled into his reserved spot near the door, Sam pulled into an empty space nearby. The sheriff never said a word. He just smiled at Sam, opening the door for him and then guiding him down a hallway to a glass door with a Burdett County Sheriff insignia on it.

"How's it going, Maureen?" Sheriff Wheeler said to the receptionist sitting at a desk in the front room. "We got any coffee ready?"

"Just made a fresh pot," Maureen said, giving Sam a smile and a nod.

The sheriff pointed at a small office off the main

room. "I'll meet you in my office," he said. "You want any coffee?"

"I'd love a cup," Sam said. "Black."

"That's the only kind we got," Wheeler replied with a chuckle.

Sam went into the office, flipped on the light and sat down in the chair across from the sheriff's desk. He scanned the room to get a sense of who he was dealing with. The sheriff had already changed Sam's plans without asking, but he had done so in a way where Sam was happy to comply. To be fair, the sheriff was right. Sam did have him on his list of contacts, but the sheriff had made some pretty broad assumptions to just commandeer Sam's day like that. It takes a certain amount of confidence to reroute a stranger so casually, and even more rare to make it feel polite.

Sam noticed a couple of pictures on the wall behind the desk. One was the sheriff holding up a large bass that he'd caught. It reminded Sam of what he was missing out on while conducting this wild goose chase. The other photo was a much younger sheriff with a younger woman and small child. No doubt, the sheriff's family.

Sheriff Wheeler walked in with two hot coffee mugs, carefully setting them both down on the desk before walking around to the other side and taking a seat. He leaned back and looked at Sam with a knowing grin. Sam could tell when he was being sized up.

"So, you're looking for Amy, huh?" the sheriff finally spoke. "I'm guessing her sister hired you."

"You'd be guessing right," Sam said. "She's having a hard time believing her sister simply left town without telling anyone."

"Except you and I both know that's probably exactly what happened," Wheeler said. "You met her husband. Would you have stuck around?"

Sam laughed. "Am I missing something? How is anyone married to that guy?"

Sheriff Wheeler grinned. "It made a lot more sense when they were right out of high school. Unfortunately, ol' Gus peaked early. He's been struggling ever since. He was a welder for a while, but he lost that job a few years back. He just got worse from there."

"And you don't think he had anything to do with Amy's disappearance?"

Sheriff Wheeler shook his head. "I do not. And I'll give you two reasons why. First, Gus is never sober enough to do anything that nefarious and not get caught. And two, Amy didn't disappear. She left town. And you strike me as someone smart enough to know that's all that happened here."

"Did you look into it at all?" Sam asked.

"Not much to look into," Wheeler explained. "Her

car is gone. Her cell phone is gone. She didn't show up for work. There ain't no reason to think this is anything more than a grown woman running away from home. Maybe it's temporary. Maybe it's for good. But there's no sense creating any fuss. You met Amy's sister, Miss Duncan. She's a bit of a ...worrier. Did she tell you her theory?"

Sam shook his head.

The sheriff grinned back. "Trust me. It's worth the listen. Just try not to laugh in her face. She's a gentle, harmless soul. Besides, I have complete confidence she ain't got a thing to worry about. There's no sense making a fuss out of it. That don't do anybody any good."

Sam tended to agree, but he felt like the sheriff was telling him to back off. And Sam did not like being told what to do.

"Still, it's probably worth checking into," Sam said. "Even just a little bit."

The Sheriff took a long sip of coffee, never taking his eyes off Sam. Finally, he agreed with another long "mmhmm".

"What it's not worth is getting the entire county all worked up and worried about someone getting murdered when there's nothing to support that," he added.

"Who said anything about murder, Sheriff?" Sam

replied. "Someone's missing. There could be lots of reasons for it. Judy Duncan asked me to see if I can figure out what that is. And if she did just leave town, to find out where she might have gone. Because that's what you do when someone goes missing."

"You keep throwing around this word 'missing,'" the sheriff countered. "You're jumping the gun a bit, son. I've lived right here in Burdett my whole life and I've seen a lot of people go. Some make a big deal about it. Others just slip away because they don't wanna be followed. Hell, people used to 'disappear' just like Amy all the time. Now with Facebook and the internet, they almost always show up somewhere else at some point or another. And you know what I say to that? God bless 'em. If she wants to leave town without telling her lowlife husband, that's her right. I'm not here to corral her back because her sister is having crazy thoughts."

Sam could feel his stubborn nature planting its feet firmly in the ground.

"I hope you're right," Sam said. "To be honest, I'm only doing my due diligence on my way to a fishing trip. Judy Duncan was not gonna take no for an answer."

The sheriff grinned. "Judy Duncan insists she has seen aliens landing behind her house. She once called 911 because Bigfoot was going through her trash. And I bet if you asked her, he had a pet Chupacabra."

"Bigfoot has a pet chupacabra?" Sam remarked. "That would actually make sense."

The sheriff smirked.

"You get my point," he said.

Sam was starting to think the sheriff made more and more sense.

"You do what you were hired to do," the sheriff continued. "It's a free country. Just do me a favor and try not to stir up dust before it's had a chance to settle. If you find out anything going on that's illegal, I'll be glad to help you out. But you and I both know, nine times out of ten the most obvious answer is the right answer. Take a look around. Try to be discreet. And then you can get on with your fishing trip."

Sam nodded. But before he could say anything he was distracted by a loud voice in the other room.

6

———

BEFORE SAM COULD TURN to the door, it was swung open by a large woman whose presence hit the room like the hot gust of air when you open an oven door. Sam figured her to be in her late 60s. Her salt and pepper hair was perfectly styled in a wavy crop cut covered in so much hairspray, it wouldn't move if it was hit by a tornado. She wore just enough makeup to be noticeable without being gaudy and a flowing purple jumpsuit draped with a silver leopard shawl. This was a woman that was not to go unnoticed.

"Sebastian, I need you to check up on something for me," she said, not even acknowledging Sam's presence.

"Miss Polly," the sheriff said. "We talked about you calling me Sheriff when I'm on duty."

Polly waved him off. "You are Sebastian to me and always will be."

The sheriff clearly had lost this argument before. He changed the subject. "Miss Polly, this here is Sam Lawson. He's a private investigator Judy Duncan hired to find her sister."

Polly turned to see Sam standing beside his chair and a concerned frown spread over her face. Her hazel eyes, bright with intelligence beneath the theatrics, softened immediately.

"Did something happen to Amy?"

Sam started to speak but the sheriff took the reins first.

"She left town is all. We were just talking about how we're all making a mountain out of a mole hill with this whole thing."

Even though what the sheriff said was true, Sam was really starting to get annoyed by the way he took over every exchange. He stuck his hand out to Polly.

"Hi. I'm Sam Lawson," he said. "And you are Polly…"

He paused, waiting for her to fill in the last name.

"You can call me Miss Polly, like everybody else," she said, taking Sam's hand into both of hers. Her grip was firm and warm, and her bracelets clinked like wind chimes. "So, do you agree? With what the sheriff said?"

Sam looked at the sheriff, who glared back to let Sam know it was in his best interest to toe the line. Sam had a hunch that this wasn't only so the sheriff could control the narrative, but also to placate the human hurricane in the room.

"He's right," Sam said. "In cases like this, it's almost always a case of the subject running away or taking off to start fresh somewhere."

"Or even to return a few days later," the sheriff quickly interjected in an effort to course-correct the conversation. "A little embarrassed but none the worse for it."

Polly let out a sigh of relief, sitting down in Sam's chair. Sam squeezed back against the wall to give her room. Polly radiated a kind of maternal authority. She was the kind of woman who could scold you and hug you in the same breath.

"I hope you're both right," Polly said. "I'd hate to think something bad had happened to one of our own. You be sure to let me know as soon as you hear anything."

The sheriff nodded. "Yes, ma'am. You know I will."

"Oh. I'm still getting complaints about those Wilkens boys," Polly said, shifting back into business mode. "They're making a lot of noise late at night and their neighbors are scared to say anything to them. I told them all you'd go give 'em a talking to."

The sheriff nodded. "I'll go over this afternoon."

"You may wanna check their trailer for drugs," Polly said. "I've heard rumors."

The sheriff nodded again. "Yes, ma'am. I'll check into it."

Sam thought he sounded less like he was placating an overly concerned citizen and more like he was taking orders from her.

Polly turned back to Sam. "Did you speak to Gus?"

It took a second for Sam to switch gears.

"Huh? Oh, the husband? Yes, ma'am." Sam nodded. "Not more than thirty minutes ago."

"He was probably already drunk as a skunk," Polly said. "Such a shame. He used to be such a fine young man. I hate he let himself go the way he has, and that he drug his sweet wife down with him."

"Do you know Amy?" Sam asked.

"Everybody in Elsip knows each other, honey," Polly said. "And we look out for each other. Although, I suppose we must have failed her in that department, for her to just take off like that."

"Well, like the sheriff said, we don't really know what happened," Sam said. "And there's certainly no reason for you to feel guilty about…"

Polly interrupted. Apparently, she wasn't finished. "I knew Amy mainly from church. She was always there to help out, bless her heart. Such a delicate little flower. I pray to the Lord that, wherever she went, she finds the peace and happiness she deserves."

Polly stood up. The room seemed to shrink an inch as she rose. "I'll get out of your hair now," she said. "It was very nice meeting you, Mr. Lawson," she said before turning to the sheriff. "You still coming over for supper tonight?"

"You know I wouldn't miss out a meal now," the sheriff said with a smile.

"You're welcome to join us, too," Polly said to Sam.

"I appreciate that," Sam said. "But I'll probably be well on my way before then."

"Well, I wish you safe travels then," Polly replied as she walked out the door, taking all the air in the room with her and leaving a soft perfume trail in her wake.

"Six o'clock, Sheriff," she yelled back over her shoulder. "Don't be late."

Sam stood in shock, feeling the vacuum of silence that Polly had left in her wake.

"Well, now you met Miss Polly," the sheriff said with a chuckle.

"She's a... a lot," Sam said, choosing his words carefully.

"Her heart is as big as her personality," the sheriff replied.

"That's pretty big," Sam replied.

No sooner had Sam sat back down than the sheriff

stood up. "I better go check on those Wilkens boys. They're probably sleeping it off right now. I'll go wake 'em up, Give 'em a taste of their own medicine."

He chuckled and walked to his door. "Where's the fishing trip?"

Sam smiled. "The southern end of Toledo Bend."

"I know some hot spots down there."

The two men walked out to the parking lot while the sheriff shared his fishing secrets, neither noticing the lone figure watching them from across the street.

7

WITH a few more people to talk to, Sam decided to take a lunch break. The sheriff had recommended Burdett's Delight, a small restaurant considered the best in town, other than the Dairy Queen.

The bell at the top of the door jangled when Sam entered, announcing his arrival to about a dozen customers who never even bothered looking up. A young waitress, about twenty, did notice him and told him he could sit anywhere. Sam looked around at the scattering of small tables and booths. Most everything was already occupied but he did spot a booth. As a bonus, it was near his truck, so he could keep an eye on his fishing gear.

He walked across the warped floor, cutting through several conversations that filled the air with small talk.

Without sampling a single bite, Sam knew he was going to love this place. The waitress met him at the booth and handed him a menu as he slid into the booth.

"What can I get you to drink?" she asked.

"I'll take a glass of tea," Sam said.

One of the things that he had always taken for granted until he traveled up north was that he didn't have to specify hot or iced tea, or sweet or unsweetened. When you ordered tea, it was assumed you meant sweet, iced tea. If you wanted anything else, you'd have to specify.

He studied the one-page menu, clearly printed on a home computer and laminated. Another benefit of a small-town restaurant: limited choices. But you could be damn sure absolutely everything on the menu was a tried-and-true winner. Sam skimmed over the selection until his eyes landed on the chicken fried steak. He didn't bother reading any further. Right on cue, the waitress returned with his iced tea and asked him if he was ready to order.

"Chicken fried steak, please," Sam said. "With extra gravy, mashed potatoes and green beans."

"You got it," the waitress said with a smile.

She darted away, only to reveal the short, chubby man who had been standing behind her. From his badge and holster, it was clear he was law enforcement.

And his black shirt tipped Sam off to what kind of law he enforced. He was a constable.

In Texas, especially rural areas, the constable is an elected peace officer that serves a specific precinct within a county. They have all the same duties and responsibilities as other law enforcement, but where the sheriff serves the entire county, a constable serves a portion of that county.

This particular constable was young. Probably in his late 20s. His Marine-style cut, and a close-cropped goatee were probably meant to help him appear older, but his big, bright eyes gave him away. Sam could tell by the stiffness of his posture and the careful way he rested his hand near his duty belt that he took his job very seriously.

"Can't do better than the chicken fried steak," the constable said.

As he slid into the booth uninvited, Sam's hopes for a quiet lunch went out the door.

"Please. Have a seat," Sam quipped.

"Sorry to barge in on your lunch," the constable said, extending his arm over the table. "I'm Constable Harlan. Clyde Harlan."

"Sam Lawson," Sam replied. "If you're stopping to pay me a visit then I'm guessing you already know why I'm here. Are you all on a group text or something?"

Clyde chuckled. A little too long and a little too hard. Sam could tell it was a nervous laugh.

"So, what can I do you for, Constable?" Sam asked.

"I seen you talking to the sheriff and I noticed Miss Polly had stopped in," Clyde said.

"Were you spying on us?" Sam asked, more amused than taken aback. Try as he might, Constable Clyde did not present an intimidating presence at all. Earnest, yes. But more like that of an overzealous Eagle Scout than a hardened law officer.

"I'm guessing the sheriff told you not to worry about Amy Booker's disappearance, right? She probably just left town for a bit. Well, don't buy it. Not for a second. Amy would never do that."

Sam perked up a bit. At least this constable had something interesting to say.

"So, you know Amy?" Sam asked.

"Since grade school. Best friends in high school up until she started dating Gus."

He practically spit out the name.

"Gus thinks she ran off with some guy named Jason Mackey," Sam said.

Clyde chuckled.

"He would," Clyde said. "Trust me. Jason ain't Amy's type. And running off with another man ain't her style. She's way too classy for that."

Sam nodded. He was beginning to think Clyde wasn't a very objective party in this whole ordeal.

"Besides, I already talked to Jason, and I checked out his place," Clyde said. "He's clean."

At least he's not lazy, Sam thought. *That already sets him apart from the other badge he'd met today.*

"And what made you feel like you needed to check out his place?" Sam asked, intrigued.

"You think you're the first person to talk to Gus?" Clyde said. "Judy called me right away and I got out to her home right away. I sure as hell knew the sheriff wasn't going to do anything."

Sam was glad to see that he was right about the sheriff's laziness.

"So, other than it being out of character, what else makes you so sure Amy didn't just leave town?" Sam asked.

Clyde leaned forward. "I'll tell you why," he said. "I found things at her house that don't make no sense. For instance, her car is gone. Okay. Fine. And her purse. Her wallet. And her phone. But her phone charger was still plugged into the wall at her house. Who takes their phone but forgets their charger?"

"You haven't met my wife," Sam deadpanned.

"What about her suitcase?" Clyde continued. "Still in her closet. Along with pretty much all her clothes."

"You did an inventory of her clothes?" Sam asked.

"I eyeballed it," Clyde said. "And Gus didn't see anything missing. Nothing but the baggy blue dress shirt and black skirt that she'd worn to work that day."

"How do you know that?"

"Because that's one of the first questions you ask when someone goes missing," Clyde said. "Her co-worker remembered. Walter Puckett. You're gonna wanna talk to him."

"Why would the sheriff be so quick to dismiss the whole thing?" Sam asked.

"Because he's allergic to anything that would make him have to actually do his job," Clyde replied.

"Who is this Miss Polly lady?" Sam asked, appreciating the honest answers.

Clyde rolled his eyes. "You could say she's the unofficial mayor of Burdett County. Or more like the Godfather."

Sam nodded. "She's that squeaky wheel that gets the oil, huh?" he asked.

Clyde grinned. "You underestimate Miss Polly at your own peril."

Both men leaned back in silence as the waitress delivered Sam's chicken fried steak and refreshed his glass of tea.

"Hey, Clyde," the waitress said. "Can I get you something?"

"Nah, I'm fixing to get out of here," Clyde said, puffing his chest a bit. "I gotta make my rounds and all."

The waitress shrugged and walked off, not as impressed as Clyde had hoped. As soon as she left, he leaned forward again, straightening the badge on his chest with two fingers, as if unconsciously reminding himself that it meant something whether anyone else believed it or not.

"Miss Polly takes care of everyone in Burdett County and everyone loves her for it, But if you do her wrong, you'll have hell to pay."

"Did Amy do her wrong?" Sam asked.

Clyde sighed and shook his head. "Amy was a sweetheart. To everyone," he said. "To a fault."

"What does that mean?" Sam asked.

"She just put up with a lot," Clyde answered.

He shifted in his seat and leaned in further, speaking in a conspiratorial whisper. "Two nights before she disappeared, at the First Baptist potluck dinner, I saw Gus laying into her. He was P.O.-pissed off, and I was about to step in when he stormed off. And before I could ask Amy if she was okay, she ran off crying."

"That would make me want to get out of town," Sam said.

Clyde shook his head. "No. You don't get it. She put up with it. She always put up with it,"

Behind the words, Sam detected the edge of guilt – the sound of a man who wished he had done more than he did.

"I'd start with Gus," Clyde said.

"I already spoke to him," Sam replied.

"Ask him about the fight," Clyde said.

"Why don't you?" Sam asked. "You're the one wearing a badge."

"With some people, this badge don't mean squat," Clyde said. "I'm not Polly-approved. Besides, Gus and I have too much history. You'd think this uniform and this badge would buy me a little respect, but I'm just that high school nerd to him. You'd probably have better luck getting anything out of him."

Constable Harlan shimmied and scooted his way out of the booth. He handed a business card to Sam.

"Let me know if you need anything," Clyde said. "You and me may be the only shot of finding out what really happened to Amy."

8

———

AFTER SCARFING down what was undeniably the best chicken fried steak he'd ever had, Sam headed back to Gus and Amy's house. While the constable clearly had tunnel vision regarding Amy, he did make some good points. And the sheriff's flat-out insistence that no harm had come to Amy — with absolutely no investigation — made him even more suspicious. As much as he wanted to get on with his fishing trip, there were still questions that needed to be answered here.

Once again, he pulled into the Booker's gravel driveway, but this time, Gus didn't rush out to meet him. Sam took advantage of the opportunity and snooped around the carport a bit. It was filled with junk that served as a Museum of Incompletion. A dozen different projects that had been started but not finished. A bicycle with no tires. A doghouse with three sides. A trolling motor with no propellor. Everything was half-done and then tossed in a heap. Sam couldn't tell if Gus lacked the skill to finish things or just the discipline. Either way, it painted a foretelling picture of a marriage that had probably suffered the same fate. Had he tossed Amy aside like another unfinished project?

Hearing a noise behind the house, Sam quietly made his way down a path that led to the backyard. Calling it a yard was quite a stretch. More of a junkyard than anything. There had been an attempt to plant some flowers near the home, but the summer heat had taken its toll on most of them. Most of the yard was red dirt with an occasional patch of dead grass. All of it was littered with spare tires, discarded furniture and a rusted steel drum filled with trash that would no doubt be burned at some point. Gus stood with his back to Sam about twenty-five yards out — still shirtless but now wearing work gloves and digging a hole with a shovel.

It was a hot afternoon. Sam figured the temperatures were clawing at 100 degrees. And Gus was drenched in sweat. Hell, Sam had worked up a sweat just walking through the carport. Why Gus chose this time of day to be doing some hard manual labor made no sense.

Unless he needed to dig a hole quick.

Sam crept toward Gus, trying to get a better look at what he was digging. From what he could tell, it was just a hole. Next to the hole, a large blue tarp had been rolled up. From the bulge it created, there was clearly something inside of it. Thankful, he had decided to bring his handgun with him, Sam put a finger on the trigger as he moved closer.

Gus stopped digging. He took off his gloves and wiped the sweat away from his drenched face. Sam took another step forward... right on to a tossed hamburger bun. The bun squished forward, causing Sam to lose his balance. He struggled to keep his footing but found himself falling back on his butt with a loud thud.

Gus spun around. "What the hell?"

Sam sat on the ground, gun in hand, and tried to act as nonchalant as possible.

"Oh, hey," Sam said. "Man, it's hot today, ain't it?"

"What are you doing out here?" Gus asked. "Is that a gun?"

Sam looked at the gun like he was surprised to see it.

"Would you look at that! Good thing the safety's on, huh?"

Sam clumsily struggled to his feet.

"What are you doing on my property?" Gus asked. "Were you sneaking up on me?"

Sam pretended to laugh. "I would definitely not call

this sneaking," he said. "I just had a few more questions I forgot to ask, and I heard you back here."

Sam tried to look over Gus's shoulder at the blue tarp.

"Sure is a hot day to be out digging a hole," Sam said.

"I like to sweat," Gus said, staring at Sam suspiciously. "Gets the toxins out of my system."

"So, you just come out here to dig? For no reason?"

"What if I did?" Gus asked. "I don't see that being any of your concern."

"You're right," Sam said. "Curious by nature. Comes with the job."

He glanced at the blue tarp again.

"You got something in that tarp?" Sam asked.

"Yeah. A big pile of none of your damn business," Gus replied.

Sam nodded, then collected himself. He held his gun in his right hand and stared back at Gus to show him he was not to be taken lightly.

"Why don't you show me?" he asked.

Gus stared back, not budging. He looked down at Sam's gun as if he was trying to calculate how much time he had before Sam could raise it and shoot.

"Why don't you see for yourself?" he finally said.

He stepped aside to allow Sam to pass. The private detective walked around Gus, being sure to stay out of his reach. When he got to the tarp, he kicked it. There was definitely something rolled up in it. Something solid. He knelt, keeping an eye on Gus and his hand on his gun.

Then he quickly yanked back the flap of the tarp. He unwrapped the contents until enough was exposed for Sam to jump up and back.

"Jesus Christ!" he yelled.

Gus laughed.

"What? You never seen a dead rabbit before?"

He took the shovel and rolled the large, bloodied animal into the hole.

"Coyotes'll dig 'em up unless I bury 'em deep."

He then took a can of coffee and poured the grounds into the hole. "This is the trick right here. Helps hide the scent."

He looked down into the hole and, satisfied with his work, looked up at Sam. He laughed.

"You should've seen your face. What'd you think you were gonna find?"

Sam didn't answer. But he had to laugh at his own stupidity.

"It sure as hell wasn't a bloody rabbit," he said. "Why don't you burn it?"

"That's just gonna attract all kinds of animals," Gus said. "No thank you."

"You really led me on there," Sam said.

"That's what you get for sneaking up on me."

The two men retreated back into the house where the window A/C unit was rattling and battling to stay ahead of the heat. Not very successfully. Gus grabbed a couple of beers, and they scooted up their chairs close to the unit.

"So did you talk to Jason?" Gus asked.

Sam shook his head. "Didn't have to. Your constable had already done it."

Gus growled. "Clyde? That boy couldn't find the bottom of a boot if it kicked him in the head."

"He said that Jason hadn't seen your wife," Sam continued. "He even searched his house. Nothing."

"That just means she's hiding good," Gus replied.

"He also told me he saw you and Amy having a fight the other night at the church. What was that all about?"

Gus shook his head.

"Clyde sees what he wants," he said. "He's had puppy eyes for Amy since junior high. But there weren't no fight."

Sam took a long pull from his beer bottle. As he did, he noticed the raw, scraped skin across Gus's knuckles – angry red marks that didn't look like they came from punching a wall.

"How'd you get those?" Sam asked, nodding toward the injuries.

Gus examined his hand, studying the red marks. Sam could tell he was buying time, thinking of how to answer.

"I punched the wall," Gus said. He pointed across the room to a big indentation in the plywood wall. "I got pissed when Amy didn't come home."

"You get pissed like that often?" Sam asked.

"What are you getting at?"

"You ever get really angry at Amy? Maybe put her in her place? Maybe your temper got the best of you and things got really out of hand?"

Gus stood.

"Get the hell out of my house."

Sam stood, raising his hands in surrender. "I'm just asking the question. It's my job.

"Well, your job is gonna get the crap knocked out of you."

Sam nodded. "It has before. I'm sure it will again."

Seeing his threats weren't ruffling the desired feathers, Gus took a second to cool down.

"Look, we got into a fight at the church, but then we came home and I apologized, and everything was fine. Hell, the next morning I even made her pancakes before she went to work."

"And that was the last time you saw her?" Sam asked.

Sam could tell the question hit Gus hard. His eyes softened and his shoulders sunk.

"Yeah," he said quietly. "It was."

"Did you know she was gonna work late?" Sam asked, not letting up.

He knew he had a window before Gus's defiance went back up and he wasn't going to miss it.

"Yeah. She told me before she left. Told me there was some fried chicken in the fridge and she'd be home by ten."

"Were you here at ten?" Sam asked.

Gus shook his head. "I didn't get home til midnight."

"You were at the bar that whole time?"

Gus nodded.

"Did she tell you why she was working late?" Sam asked.

Gus scowled. "No."

"Did you ask?"

"Some county stuff, I guess," Gus said. "I don't know. Maybe she was off with Jason Mackey, like I said."

Sam stood. "Thanks for the beer," he said. "Unfortunately, it looks like there are some other people I need to talk to."

9

SAM LEFT the Booker house and headed back to Burdett, kicking himself the whole way that he didn't stop at the County Courthouse when he was right there. He was chasing rumors instead of steering his own investigation, and it was costing him daylight. And precious fishing time.

He pulled into the parking lot, making a mental note to find out where Amy's car had been parked. Surely, the building had security cameras. It's something the sheriff should have checked already as a matter of protocol. But Sam was already learning that things didn't operate by any kind of standard procedure in Burdett County.

He walked in the main doors, taking note of the

security cameras positioned at the doorway and another facing the parking lot.

Bingo.

It was not likely that any county security department would turn over any recordings to a private investigator – especially one from out of town, but Constable Clyde could probably get them. Sam walked through the main foyer. It was late afternoon but, with not a soul in sight, the building already seemed shut down.

He followed the directions to the County Records office and was relieved to see someone moving behind the frosted glass door. He opened it to find a small, round man standing behind a counter. He was probably mid-40s, with thinning hair, a full mustache and wire-framed glasses. He was leaning in front of a computer, typing furiously. And even though he was intensely focused on the screen, Sam couldn't help but pick up on his jittery, nervousness.

"I'll be right with you," the man said.

Sam waited patiently and took in the office. It wasn't a large space. Two desks faced each other in the center of the room with walls of file cabinets and bookshelves lining each wall. Sam assumed the desks belonged to Amy and her boss, Walter Puckett. And the man frantically pecking at a computer keypad had to be Walter.

Both desks were meticulously neat and organized. So much so, that Sam wondered if they were actually used at all. From the few personal items on the desks, Sam figured the one on the left, with more colorful desk accessories, was Amy's.

The face-to-face arrangement of the desks reminded him of a similar office layout back when he was a police detective. Supposedly, it was incredibly efficient. Sam had always found it pretty intrusive, having to stare right at a co-worker all day, every day. But Sam wound up making a good friend that way. In fact, he was one of the friends meeting him for the fishing trip.

He wondered if Walter and Amy had built that same kind of bond. The kind you can only get from staring at each other for hours every day.

"So sorry," the frantic man said. "I'm shorthanded the last couple of days and I'm realizing how little I know about things."

"Are you Walter Puckett?" Sam asked.

The man paused and looked up at Sam, the color draining from his face. "I am," he said.

"I was wondering if I could borrow a few minutes of your time to talk about Amy Booker."

Walter's face twisted with panic, and he started gasping for air.

"Oh, God," he said. "You found her. I knew it. I knew it."

He grabbed a chair and fell back into it. "Is she... is she... dead?"

"Why did you hear something?" Sam asked, now just as panicked.

Walter looked at Sam, confused.

"I thought... you said."

"I don't know anything," Sam said. "I was gonna ask you what you knew!"

"Who are you?" Walter asked.

Sam, seemingly oblivious to the mild heart attack he had just given Walter, held out his hand.

"I'm a private investigator," Sam explained. "Amy's sister hired me to look into her disappearance."

Walter let out a deep sigh and started taking deep breaths as he shook Sam's hand.

"You scared me to death. I thought you were here to tell me..."

He leaned forward, hands on his knees to catch his breath.

"Sorry about that," Sam said. "You okay?"

Walter nodded. He slowly caught his breath, grabbed a cup of water and took a large gulp.

"Wait. You're a private eye?" he asked with renewed energy. "Do you have any theories? Any suspects?"

"So, I take it you're not buying the 'just left town' theory?" Sam asked.

"No way," Walter said, fully animated. "Amy wouldn't take off without saying goodbye. When I left work the other day, she told me 'I'll see you tomorrow.' Why say that if she wasn't planning on coming in? She even reminded me it was my day to bring in coffee. We take turns picking up coffee in the morning."

Sam asked all the standard questions. Had Walter noticed anything unusual? Had Amy talked about needing to get away? Trouble at home? Enemies? Walter's answers were dead ends. Everything seemed business as usual with the young woman. She definitely had marital issues, but she hadn't acted like they were so bad she needed to sneak away.

"Just look at her desk," Walter said. "She was so organized. But she had written a to-do list for her next day. Why would she write that if she was planning on leaving town?"

To throw everyone off? Sam wondered.

As Walter talked, Sam took note of his mannerisms. The man couldn't complete a sentence without adjusting something – straightening, aligning, nudging objects into perfect rows. He'd even arranged the pencils by height.

"Amy loved her job," Walter said, absentmindedly straightening files in a staggered holder. "She actually loved filing things. And she was fascinated by the county's history. Always staying late looking through old records — just for fun. Can you imagine? That's what she was doing the night she went missing."

Sam perked up. "What kind of records?"

"Oh, you name it. She'd go through different phases," Walter said, standing and walking over to her desk. "I think lately she'd been digging through land deeds. Tracing family history through property ownership. It's a small town, and most people are living in the same house their great grandparents lived in."

"Do you know if she found anything interesting?" Sam asked.

Walter laughed. "To her, definitely. To you and me? Probably not so much."

"Do you have the files she was looking at?" Sam asked.

Walter shook his head. "She always put everything back. She wrote it all down in her journal. Had this little pink leather journal. She was always scribbling into it. And before you ask, I already looked for it here."

Walter grew solemn. "I'm so thankful you're looking into this. The sheriff isn't taking it seriously."

"Well, you'll be glad to know your constable is."

"No offense," Walter said, "But Clyde doesn't do much more than issue speeding tickets and help with warrants and stuff. Constables may do more in other counties, but the Sheriff handles pretty much everything here. Clyde's more like a... mascot."

Sam remembered the way the waitress treated him at the diner.

Yeah. Mascot fit.

"I guess there's not enough crime in Burdett County for two peace officers," Walter said with a shrug.

Sam stood. "Well, there may be now."

Walter shut his eyes and shook his head. "Do you really think something bad has happened to Amy?"

Sam considered the question. The only thing he knew for sure was that there were too many unanswered questions. As much as he hated it, he was going to have to put his fishing trip on hold. At least for a day.

"I don't know," Sam finally answered. "But I promise you I'm going to find out. And I'm gonna start by taking a look at this building's security footage."

10

———

AS SAM HAD EXPECTED, the building security head wasn't willing to share the security footage with just anyone. But Sam had called Constable Clyde in advance and didn't have to wait long for the "law enforcement mascot" to show up. After a short side conversation, Clyde motioned for Sam to follow him to the Head of Security's office.

Kenny Gladstone quickly typed in a few specifications and turned his monitor so all three of them could see the screen. It was split into eight views, all of them showing grainy black and white footage of hallways and doorways. All but one.

"Why is that one black?" Sam asked, putting his finger on the monitor's black quadrant.

Gladstone slapped his hand away.

"Unfortunately, that is the camera pointing to the parking lot," he said. "It hasn't worked in a long time."

"And you didn't bother fixing it?" Sam asked.

Gladstone shot him a glare. "It's on the list."

He turned back to the monitor and pressed the space bar to fast forward through the footage. Other than the main hallway, there was little if any activity.

"I cued it up to right before closing," Gladstone said.

As if on cue, people began to appear on screen as they left their offices. The hallway filled up as people began to leave the building.

"There's Walter Pucket," Gladstone said, pointing to a quadrant where Walter could be seen walking out a door, but not before saying something to someone still inside.

"Probably saying goodnight to Amy," Clyde said. "That means she's still inside."

After the last few stragglers emptied out of the building, the videos grew still again.

"This goes on for about four hours until right around nine," Gladstone said, pointing to the quadrant where Walter had been seen earlier. "Then Mrs. Booker shows up here."

Sure enough. Amy walked out of the door to the County Records office and locked it behind her. She looked around and then headed on her way.

Sam noted what she was wearing: An oversized sweater over a sundress and plain flats.

"Why a sweater?" Sam asked. "It wasn't even chilly that night."

"Offices can get pretty cold," Gladstone said. "I wear my jacket most days."

Sam nodded as they continued to watch.

"She looks nervous," Clyde said.

"That's what everyone looks like when they leave the building late," Gladstone said. "It's a creepy place at night."

"Was there any security on hand? Sam asked.

"No, sir," Gladstone replied. "We leave at six and don't show up again until 7 in the morning."

They all watched the footage until they spotted Amy again, looking behind her as she walked briskly down the hallway.

"She's acting like someone is following her," Sam said.

"Folks get twitchy in this building at night. Lots of echoes playing tricks on you," Gladstone said. "I assure you, if I pulled footage from another night she worked late, she'd be acting the same way."

He pointed to a different quadrant on the monitor. "There. Now she's at the front door."

In the footage, Amy locks the front door behind her

and looks out toward the parking lot, almost hesitating before she walks out of frame.

Gladstone turned to the two men. "Like I said, not much there."

While Clyde thanked Gladstone for his help, Sam kept his eyes glued on the footage. Then he saw something that caught his attention.

"Hold up," he said. "Can you back that up a little bit?"

Surprised, Gladstone rewound the footage slowly.

"There," Sam said, pointing at a light shining at the front entrance. "What's that?"

Gladstone studied it for a second to be sure. "Just her headlights."

"Go back again," Sam said.

Gladstone complied, replaying the footage.

"The lights move," Sam said. "They come in at an angle before they stop."

Clyde and Gladstone looked at Sam, waiting for an explanation.

"If she just got in her car and turned on her lights, they'd suddenly appear," Sam said. "But these lights seem to be arriving to the parking lot."

"Maybe someone picked her up?" Clyde asked.

"But her car wasn't here the next day, right?" Sam asked.

"I got here at 6:55 and there were no cars in the parking lot," Gladstone answered.

"Keep playing the footage," Sam said.

They all watched as the headlights seemingly shown into the building. Finally, they moved out of frame.

"That's her leaving," Gladstone said.

"Keep rolling," Sam said.

There was no movement for another two hours. Then a set of headlights swerved in again at about the same location.

"What's this?" Clyde asked, leaning forward.

After a minute and a half, it looked like another set of headlights suddenly appeared. As soon as they did, the first pair of lights veered away. Then the second set of headlights veered away in the same pattern.

"Holy shit," Clyde said.

"So, she left with someone and then came back later?" Gladstone asked.

"That's one possibility," Sam said. "All we can safely say is that another car pulled into the driveway as Amy walked toward her car, and that car left. Then a car returned two hours later, left again, followed by Amy's car."

"Who was in that second car?" Clyde asked.

11

———————

HAVING GIVEN up on meeting his fishing buddies, at least for one night, Sam asked directions to the closest motel—which was an old Super 8 thirty miles out of town. Not wanting to leave his fishing gear unattended overnight, Sam spent another thirty minutes untying his labyrinth of bungee cords and rope, then hauling everything into his room.

Usually, Sam wasn't particular at all about where he stayed. A door, a mattress and a toilet were his only requirements. But this particular Super 8 had seen better days. Stale cigarette smoke had buried itself in the yellow curtains and dark red carpet. Bleach had clearly been used to clean up God-knows-what. Luckily, Sam had his sleeping bag, so he could avoid sliding in between the sheets that could probably tell some terrifying stories he would rather not know about. And even though water seeped out of the shower head in nothing more than a trickle, it was warm, and Sam was able to wash off the day. He plopped onto one of the full-size beds in the room and grabbed his phone.

Carla picked it up after one ring.

"Hey, you," she said. "How did it all go?"

"It's still going," Sam said, not trying to hide his disappointment.

"So, you think you've got a legitimate case?" she asked.

"It's definitely not as cut and dry as I had hoped," Sam replied. "There are a lot of unanswered questions, and the local sheriff is exactly how Judy described him —not even the least bit concerned. I can't decide if he's laid back or lazy."

"Or maybe covering up something?" Carla asked.

"Or, for someone. Or maybe he's afraid of any truth he might find."

Sam slid down on the bed. Hearing his wife's voice instantly relaxed him. "I'm going to talk to a few more people tomorrow but, after that, I honestly don't know what good I can do here."

"Do you really think that? Or are you trying to make excuses so you can go fishing?"

Sam smirked. His wife knew him too well.

"Probably a little of both," he admitted. "So how was your day?"

"Oh, it was amazing," Carla said, the tone of her voice instantly energetic. "You're not going to believe this one body that came in."

Sam smiled as his wife described, in clinical detail, the body she had to examine that day. It was a male, mid-50s, who had been found by his adult nephew after apparently dying in his favorite recliner, remote in one hand and a beer in the other,

"How and why he didn't drop the beer can or the remote is fascinating," Carla said.

"Now that's the way to go," Sam said. "What was the cause of death?"

"Brain aneurism," Carla answered. "He died instantly."

Carla went on to explain how she determined the cause of death using words that Sam couldn't begin to understand. But he didn't care. He just loved the sound of her voice, hearing how much she loved her job and how good she was at it. He envied her passion.

A knock at the door made Sam jump. He got up and looked out the peephole.

"Hon, I'm gonna need to call you back," he said.

He opened the door to Constable Clyde.

"Oh, good. You're still up," Clyde said, letting himself into the room.

"By all means, come in," Sam muttered.

"I've been thinking about this whole Amy case and it's just not sitting right with me," Clyde said as he paced the room.

"Yeah, we already established that," Sam said. "That's why we're looking into it."

Clyde looked around the room. "This place is a dump," he said. "You know, you can stay at my place. I've got a pull-out couch."

"I'm fine," Sam said. "Why are you here?"

"I thought it'd be a good idea to map out tomorrow's game plan," Clyde said. "So, we can hit the ground running."

Sam had to laugh at Clyde's assumed partnership, but he certainly wasn't going to refuse the assist.

"Why don't we do that over coffee?" Sam asked. "In the morning?"

Clyde shook his head. "Now works better for me. While all the thoughts are still running around in my head."

Sam slumped down in a chair with a sigh. He motioned for Clyde to take a seat at the foot of the bed.

"So, what do you propose?" Sam asked. The question was ripe with resignation.

"Well, between the two of us we've already talked to

most of the key players, right?" Clyde asked as he sat down.

"I still want to talk to that guy Gus accused of having an affair with Amy," Sam replied.

"Jason Mackey? I already talked to him," Clyde said. "It's a dead-end."

"Granted. But I still want to talk to him. If Gus suspects him, he must have some connection with Amy. Maybe he knows something that can point us in the right direction."

Clyde shook his head. "I really don't think so."

"Well, what do you propose?"

"There's a lot of people in town that deal with Amy," Clyde said. "Either through her church or volunteer stuff she does. I say we start with them. I made a list."

He pulled a notepad out of his chest pocket and ripped a page out for Sam.

"It's just some key people," Clyde said. "But maybe they can point us in the right direction."

"You know where to find these people?" Sam asked.

"That's part of my job," Clyde said, puffing his chest a bit.

"Okay, how about this?" Sam proposed. "I'll pay a visit to Jason Mackey first thing, then I'll meet you at Burdett's Delight for coffee and we can go through the people on your list."

Clyde started to object to the Jason Mackey part of

the deal, but realized Sam wasn't going to back down. He nodded.

"Fine. 7 a.m. sharp at Burdett's," he said.

"8:30 a.m.," Sam countered. "Let's give people a chance to wipe the sleep out of their eyes."

12

———

Sam started the next day with a visit to Jason Mackey's house. He caught the young man right as he was leaving for work and could see why Gus was jealous of him. Dark hair, blue eyes and in great shape, he could rouse up just about any man's insecurities. Unfortunately, the conversation was a complete nothing burger.

Jason let out a tired sigh when Sam introduced himself and immediately asked if Gus had accused him of stealing his wife away. He went on to say, that in addition to the constable's visit, Gus had been harassing him for months. He was at the point where he was thinking about getting a restraining order.

"It's more than annoying," Jason said. "He's showing up where I work and trying to pick fights. I'd probably have been fired by now if my boss didn't know what a nut job Gus is."

Jason told him that he only knew Amy from high school but hadn't spoken a word to her since. He'd see her every once in a while, which was only natural in such a small community. But she wasn't even a blip on his radar. He told Sam he was welcome to go check out his house. The door was unlocked.

Sam could tell this was a dead-end and didn't want to waste either one of their time, but he did ask Jason a few more questions.

"So, when you saw Amy, was she alone? With Gus? With someone else?"

Jason shrugged. "I honestly don't remember. Sometimes she was alone. Eating her lunch and reading a book or something. One time, she was with a group of people. Looked like they worked together. I honestly don't remember."

Sam thanked him for his time and gave him a card, asking him to call if he thought of anything at all.

With that bit of due diligence out of the way, Sam made his way to Burdett's for a much-needed cup of coffee. Clyde was already there with a map of the area spread out over the table. Before Sam could sit down, Clyde started to lay out his plan.

"I marked the route from Amy's house to her job," Clyde said. "Most of the area on the path is woods, but there are a couple of houses along the way. I figure we could hit those first."

Then he pointed to an area he had circled in red.

"There's also some houses right off the main road. Over here," he said. "It backs up to McKinney Creek. Might be worth talking to a few folks there, too."

Sam nodded, resigned to the fact that Clyde had already decided their game plan. He hoped they'd be able to bang out these interviews by noon. Sam still held on to the notion that he'd be able to join his fishing trip later in the day, but it was beginning to seem more and more like a pipe dream.

Clyde and Sam began knocking on doors, but no one seemed to know anything. While most people knew who Amy was, they hadn't seen her lately. And no one saw her car or anything suspicious on the night she disappeared. On top of the lack of useful information, the canvassing was taking longer than expected. Mainly because of good ol' Texas hospitality. No matter which door they knocked on, they were invited in for coffee.

More than one house offered them breakfast. One elderly couple insisted on giving each of them a napkin full of bacon.

As noon crept up on them, they had completed most of the houses along the main highway. Next stop was a sub-division called Cypress Meadows. Clyde had told him it was a collection of old homes built for factory workers back in the day. They were slowly falling apart and most of them were empty, but a few of them still had people living in them. Sam wondered how many of those people would actually be home on a weekday, but Clyde reassured him that most of them were either retired or unemployed.

"Cypress Meadows is like our own little assisted living community – without the assistance," Clyde explained as they rolled off the state highway on to a dirt road. "Retired people with no savings, or people that lost their job when the tire factory shut down five years ago. People that can't afford to move. A few of the homes are almost halfway homes for people that hit a rough spot and just need to get their footing back.

"Miss Polly owns a bunch of the houses," he continued. "When people were facing foreclosure or they hit hard times, she'd take over the mortgage to help them out."

"Is Miss Polly rich?" Sam asked.

"Wealth is relative. By lots of standards, I'd say no.

But in this community, she is Queen Polly. She's always given back, though. She used to have some trailer homes parked behind her house where she let people stay while they got their life together. Then, when her husband passed, she sold his farm and feed company and uses that money to help others out."

"That's impressive," Sam replied.

"She's bailed out this community more than once," Clyde said. "But don't let that fool you. As charitable as she can be, she don't take shit from no one. She's a hard cookie and holds everyone up to high standards. People don't just love her. They respect her."

"Maybe even fear her?" Sam asked with a grin.

Clyde chuckled. "Absolutely. You don't want Miss Polly on your bad side. Believe you me."

They pulled off the dirt road on to a side road that led into woods. About a mile down this new road, the trees began to open up, revealing a scattering of run-down homes on either side. Sam had half expected a clean community with new housing units and fresh grass. But this looked more like slum housing. The houses were old and falling apart and sat uncomfortably close to each other. The land around the homes was overrun with weeds and tall grass. The dirt road wound around the homes and trees so Sam could only see six or seven homes at a time.

"It don't look like much," Clyde said. "But to these

people, it's home. And it's a helluva lot better than being homeless."

Sam silently agreed. Like Clyde had said, wealth is relative.

As Clyde pulled on to the shoulder of the road and killed the engine, Sam noticed a few old people sitting in folding camp chairs in front of their homes, all staring at the constable's car as it rolled into their community.

"Let's get this over with," Sam said, not expecting anything to come from people that lived this far off the main road. He opened his door, immediately slapped in the face by the sticky midday heat. "You want to split up, cut our time in half?"

"I think it's best we stick together," Clyde said. "Some of these people may not take kindly to a stranger nosing around in their business."

13

SAM CHECKED HIS WATCH. It was closing in on two o'clock and they were finally coming up on the last cluster of homes. So far, their search had yielded nothing of interest. Even the people that recognized Amy didn't really know her and none had seen her on the day she went missing. One pattern that did emerge, however, was the power of Polly. Sam had quickly learned that simply mentioning her name made people perk up. They all spoke about her with a sort of weird reverence. Granted, she had given many of these people a second lease on life. The so-called rent she charged was based entirely on what a person could afford. And she gave a lot of leeway on due dates – an expression he heard over and over again was "I don't know how I'd have made it if it weren't for Miss Polly. She saved my life."

Partly because of her benevolence and probably because of her dominating personality, Miss Polly was clearly the unofficial 'Governor of Burdett County.' Any judge, mayor or law enforcement, including the Sheriff, were merely figureheads.

As they approached the first home in the cluster, an elderly African American woman opened the door before Clyde could knock.

"I seen y'all coming, Officer," the woman said with a gentle smile. "Knocking on all them doors. Thought I'd give those knuckles a little break."

Clyde smiled. "I appreciate that Mrs. Garrett."

The woman waved Clyde off. "I'm not your teacher no more, Clyde Harlan. You can call me Lila Mae."

Realizing this woman was one of Clyde's teachers, Sam now noticed how shy and self-conscious the constable was suddenly acting.

"You were one of Clyde's teachers?" Sam asked.

Lila Mae nodded. "Sixth grade Texas history. And eighth grade science."

"I bet you were everyone's favorite," Sam said, trying to charm the woman. But Lila Mae laughed as she shook her head.

"Oh, I was mean as a snake," she said. "That's the

only way to get through to pre-teen boys. But Clyde here was always a good student."

"Teacher's pet. Teacher's pet," Sam said, playfully needling Clyde.

Lila Mae's face turned stone cold serious.

"Don't you make fun of a man for being respectful of his teacher," she said.

Sam looked down, feeling like a chastised sixth grader.

"It's okay, Mrs. Garrett. I mean, Lila Mae," Clyde said, "I can vouch for this one."

Lila Mae looked Sam up and down suspiciously and shook her head. Then she broke out in a loud laugh.

"I'm just messing with you," she said to Sam. "If I was serious, I'd already have taken a switch to you. Now what is it I can do for y'all?"

Clyde asked Lila Mae about Amy. Sam's attention drifted and he looked around the cluster of homes. Thick woods sat about twenty feet behind them. If Sam remembered right from the map Clyde had shown him earlier, a large creek ran back there. He unfortunately knew that was an area they would most likely search— if Amy remained missing and if the sheriff declared her missing. Two very big ifs.

Something moved among the trees, catching Sam's attention. As he looked in the area of the movement, an old hound came loping out of the thicket. It was brown and black with a streak of white from under its chin to the bottom of its chest. Its tongue swung out of the side of its mouth as it loped along the tree line, its tail pointed straight up.

That's when Sam became aware of a man half-hidden in the woods, staring in Sam's direction. For all Sam knew, he'd been there the whole time. The man noticed Sam staring and he stepped back out of sight. Sam heard a whistle but, if the man was calling the dog, the dog wasn't listening.

"There's a man in the woods," Sam said, interrupting Clyde mid-sentence.

"Excuse me?" Clyde asked.

"I just saw a man in the woods there. And a dog," Sam said again.

Lila Mae nodded her head.

"That's ol' Skeeter," she said. "He lives back in there. By the creek. His cornbread ain't done in the middle, but he's harmless. That dog, on the other hand, keeps digging up my flowers."

As she spoke, the dog came bounding his way toward them. Sam could see it had something in his mouth.

"Get on out, now!' Lila Mae yelled at the dog. "Gitt!"

But the dog paid the same amount of attention to Lila Mae that it did to the man in the woods.

"What's that in its mouth?" Clyde asked.

He crouched down to coax the dog over.

"Hey, buddy. Whatcha got there?" Clyde said in a sing-song voice.

The dog noticed Clyde and started loping toward him. As he got closer, it became clear that he was carrying a chewed-up shoe. The dog happily traded his prize for fresh rubs under the chin. As Clyde rubbed the dog's droopy face, he took the shoe and began to examine it, being careful to touch as little of it as possible.

"Sam, you need to take a look at this."

Sam crouched next to Clyde and they both examined the shoe. It was a women's brown leather flat — the same type of shoe Amy had been wearing the night she went missing.

14

CLYDE PLACED the shoe on the hood of his SUV to get a better look.

"Nobody touch it," he shouted at the crowd that had gathered around him.

"That looks like blood," an old man commented, pointing at a stain on the shoe.

"That's too orange for blood," another said.

While the locals argued over the proper color of blood on an old shoe, Sam pulled out his phone to call the sheriff.

"You don't need to call him," Clyde said. "I've got this under control."

"He still needs to know. He's gonna have to take Amy's disappearance seriously now," Sam said.

He looked around.

"Where'd the dog go?" he asked.

Sam and Clyde scanned the area. The dog was nowhere to be seen.

"Anyone see where the dog went?" Clyde yelled.

The crowd looked around as well. They had all been so transfixed by the chewed-up shoe, no one had paid any attention to the hound.

"He's probably back down by the creek with ol' Skeeter," one old-timer suggested.

"We need to find that dog," Sam said. "Find out where he got that shoe."

"I know the creek better," Clyde said, bolting off toward the creek before Sam could respond.

Sam stood in front of the shoe, blocking it from the curious crowd. The afternoon sun was almost as unbearable as the humidity. He used both hands to wipe the sweat from his face. He thought of his friends. They were probably all in the cabin, seeking refuge from the heat after a morning of fishing. He'd like to think they were missing Sam a little, but truth be told, he'd been away from the force for so long now, they probably had all but forgotten he was supposed to join them.

Sam didn't have much time to feel sorry for himself before the Sheriff pulled up next to Clyde's SUV. He took his time getting out of his vehicle. Sam knew it was more of a power play than anything. Finally, the tall man casually sauntered over to Sam.

"So, whaddaya got here?" he asked.

Sam could practically feel the condescension in his voice. Like he was dealing with a couple of kids who swore they'd seen Bigfoot.

"You tell me," Sam said. "This shoe matches the description of what Amy was wearing on the night she was missing."

The sheriff held the shoe up to examine it.

"That's a pretty common kind of shoe," he said. "And it's pretty chewed-up."

"You ever have a dog?" Sam asked.

"Of course," the sheriff replied.

"Then you know it only takes a few minutes for them to completely destroy a shoe."

The sheriff looked around.

"Where's Clyde?" he asked.

"He went looking for the dog," Sam said. "And to see what else might be down by the creek."

"Whose dog?" the sheriff asked.

"It was Skeeter's old hound," Lila Mae chimed in. "He came running up here with that thang all balled up in his mouth."

"Where's Skeeter?" the sheriff asked.

"Clyde's looking for him, too," Sam answered.

The sheriff examined the shoe again. He touched the red stain with a finger and then brought his finger to his tongue.

"I don't think this is blood," he said.

"What else could it be?" Sam asked.

"Rust stain," the sheriff answered. "From the dirt. Especially if this was down by the creek. Lots of red clay out here."

Sam felt stupid. He knew the dirt in East Texas was rich with iron. And when it was exposed to air and water, it would easily oxidize, creating rust. If the shoe had been stuck down in the clay mud, it's very likely it picked up a stain. Sam had been so excited in finding a break in the case, he had rushed into an assumption. It was a rookie mistake that he couldn't afford to make with the sheriff.

"Still should be sent out for testing," Sam said, trying to maintain some credibility. "We could get a DNA sample from it to prove it's Amy's."

The sheriff sighed. "Or prove it ain't. But it'll take weeks before we get something back."

"Well, then we better get on it," Sam said. "We need to go out there and help Clyde search the creek."

Before the Sheriff could reply, an old, gold Cadillac barreled up behind the sheriff's SUV. Sam couldn't see the driver but heard the door open then slam shut. Then he heard her voice.

"What did you find, Sebastian?"

Both Sam and the sheriff let out audible groans. It was Miss Polly.

15

THE SHERIFF TOOK a step forward as Miss Polly barreled around the corner of his SUV. He put out his arms to stop her, but he might as well have been trying to stop a freight train.

"Miss Polly, I told you I'd call you if there was anything to see here," he said.

"Well, y'all all are sure as hell looking at something," she said, brushing past him toward the shoe that still sat on the constable's SUV.

As soon as she saw it, she stopped in her tracks.

"Oh, Lord All Mighty. Please don't let that be what it looks like."

She took a step back and started to lose her balance. The sheriff and a couple of the men from the crowd rushed to hold her steady. Sam thought it was a bit over the top but, he had to admit the sorrow that had washed over Polly's face seemed genuine.

"You think that's..." she couldn't finish the question.

"Now, Miss Polly, it's probably not. That's a pretty common kind of shoe and we don't know how long it's been out here."

"What's that big ol' stain?" Polly asked, pointing a wide circle toward the shoe.

"I'm pretty sure it's rust. From rocks down by the creek," the sheriff offered.

Polly nodded her head, latching on to that explanation.

"He's gonna have it tested. For DNA," Sam said, shooting a glance at the sheriff.

A scrawny young man rushed over with a folding lawn chair and opened it for Polly.

"Oh, bless you, son," she said as the man and another helped gently maneuver her large frame into the seat. Sam marveled at how everyone seemed to revere this woman.

"Where'd you find it?" Polly asked.

"That ol' hound Boone brought it up from over on the tree line," Lila Mae said.

"Skeeter's dog?" Polly asked.

"Yes, ma'am," Lila Mae answered. "I was talking to Clyde and this fella here when he come running up like he had a stick in his mouth, but it turned out being this shoe."

"That damn dog may have finally done something good," Polly said. "Where are all of them?"

No one was sure enough of what she meant to answer the question.

Polly explained herself with more than a touch of frustration. "The dog. Skeeter. Clyde. Where are they?"

"The dog ran off and the constable went after him," Sam said.

"Well, why don't you go down there and help him?" Miss Polly directed. "Take a group of men with you so y'all can spread out."

Sam found himself nodding and jumping into action as if he'd been given an order by his sergeant. It was only while watching Polly pick out a group of men to help him that he realized how quickly he had fallen under her spell. And she had completely taken over.

"You coming?" Sam asked the sheriff.

"I need to get that shoe out to the lab," he answered with a wink. "The sooner I send it out, the sooner we'll have answers."

"That's a good idea, Sheriff," Polly agreed.

"The answer may be right beyond those trees," Sam argued.

Miss Polly glared at him. She clearly was not used to anyone questioning her.

"You got enough men to help you, and I'm praying to God y'all all come up empty handed," she said sternly. "I don't want to have lost any time if that's the case."

Sam nodded.

"You go help Clyde and let the sheriff do his job," she continued. "That sound alright to you?"

Sam knew it was a question that did not need an answer. The point was made. Sam wasn't law enforcement and had no real jurisdiction. Granted, neither did she, even though it was very clear she was in charge. Still, there was no way Sam was going to get caught in a power struggle that he could not win. He needed to focus on what was important.

Finding Amy Booker.

Miss Polly motioned for help and a couple of men took her arms so she could stand. She walked right up to Sam and spoke softly in his face.

"I'll tell you something else. You see Skeeter, you be careful. That man ain't nothing but trouble and if any foul play has fallen upon Amy, I can guaran-damn-tee you that he had something to do with it."

16

———

Since the other five men knew the area better, Sam let them lead the search to the creek. One of them, Toby Clague, volunteered to take charge and pointed to different points in the woods for each man to take.

As they began to fan out, Sam found himself wondering if they were prepared for what they might find. If the shoe was Amy's, and that was a blood stain, then any discovery was sure to be gruesome. Sam hoped against hope that the sheriff was right, but his gut knew better. And he knew the sheriff knew better, too. So why the reluctance on his part? Was he in denial about what it might mean? Naive about the possibility? Sam had done a little research before taking the case and Burdett County hadn't had a murder in thirty years. That's longer than the sheriff's entire tenure.

Maybe he was afraid. Since he'd never handled a murder case, he wasn't sure what to do. But he could easily call in support if that were the case. Of course, that would be admitting he needed help, and it was clear the sheriff was a proud man. Still, Sam didn't think he was so proud as to jeopardize a woman's life.

And then there was the Miss Polly factor. The sheriff clearly wasn't really in charge. Miss Polly ran the show in Burdett County. But maybe that was because no one else was stepping up to do the job. She seemed genuinely concerned about Amy. And the way she directed Sam to take some men and search the creek while the sheriff submitted the shoe to the forensics lab was exactly the best thing to do, given the circumstances. As Sam walked through the wild switchgrass, scanning left to right with every step, he decided Miss Polly was the advocate he needed, not the sheriff.

Sam reached the tree line about the same time as the other men and, as they stepped into the woods, they all disappeared from each other's sight. The woods were thick and blocked the afternoon sun. Sam welcomed the drop in temperature that came with the shade but, without a breeze, the humidity was as oppressive as ever. Sam trudged slowly over a cushion of pine needles and moss, occasionally stepping over a fallen tree trunk, peering back to check for a hidden body. As he got closer to the creek, he heard the rustle of brush and the sound of twigs breaking. Something was coming toward him. He spun around to the sounds just as Boone bounded toward him.

Sam let out the adrenaline with a loud sigh and knelt to greet the dog. Boone lifted his head and shut his eyes, welcoming the scratches behind his ears and under his chin. Then Sam heard another loud CRACK. He looked up to see an old man standing over him.

Skeeter Wells glared down at Sam. Sam, kneeling on one leg, was at a clear disadvantage. His instinct was to stand up, but he didn't want Skeeter to take that as a sign of aggression. So, he stayed kneeling and petting the dog, pretending like Skeeter's presence was no big deal.

"This your dog?" Sam asked.

"Who are you?" Skeeter asked.

Sam took the question as an opportunity to stand. He extended his hand. "I'm Sam. Sam Lawson."

Skeeter looked at Sam's hand but made no effort to shake it.

"What are you doing with my dog?" he asked.

"Just petting him," Sam said. "I love old hounds."

Skeeter made a clicking sound with his tongue and Boone stepped back next to him.

"He's not yours," Skeeter said.

"Oh, I was just petting him," Sam said. "I wouldn't dare take another man's dog."

Skeeter squinted at Sam, studying him. Sam did the same. The old man's face was buried underneath a bushy white beard and knotted, curly hair. His weathered skin was marked with deep wrinkles, and a heavy, furrowed brow cast a shadow over his dark eyes. Still, Sam could see a sadness in them.

"You was up by the homes earlier," Skeeter said.

"I was," Sam replied. "And you were out by the tree line. Your dog brought me a present. A brown leather shoe. You know anything about that?"

Skeeter looked down at his dog.

"What you done dug up this time?" he asked Boone, then looked back up to Sam. "He's a good dog but he's always digging stuff up. Gets us both in a lot of trouble."

"Yeah, well this time he grabbed a shoe that looked like it had blood on it," Sam said, deciding to lean into the unproven blood theory to see if it got a reaction.

"Blood?" Skeeter asked.

He shook his head and started to walk away.

"Well, it looked like blood," Sam said, realizing he didn't want Skeeter to put his defenses up so quickly. "We're not sure yet."

But Skeeter walked past Sam as if he was done with the conversation. Sam trotted after him.

"Do you know where he got it?" Sam asked.

"I don't know where he finds half the stuff he does," Skeeter mumbled.

Sam continued to follow as Skeeter led Boone down to the creek where the dog began to immediately lap up the still, muddy water. Skeeter knelt and scooped up a handful for himself.

"You know Amy Booker?" Sam asked.

"I don't know most people," Skeeter answered.

Sam pulled up a picture of Amy on his phone and showed it to Skeeter. He saw the old man's face immediately soften before he quickly looked away.

"Why you showing me that?" he asked.

"Do you know her?" Sam asked again.

"Why do you wanna know?" Skeeter asked back, his voice growing louder and angry.

Sam held out the picture, forcing the question. But the old man turned his back to Sam.

"She's missing," Sam said. "You know anything about that?"

Sam could see Skeeter's back tighten. He curled his hands into fists and squeezed so hard his arms shook.

Then he calmed himself and turned around slowly. He grabbed the Sam's phone out of his hands and looked at the picture again. Sam wasn't sure but he thought he saw tears in the old man's eyes.

"Did something happen to her?" Skeeter asked quietly.

"That's what we're trying to figure out," Sam said. "You know her, don't you?"

Skeeter nodded, never taking his eyes off her image. "She was such a good soul," he said. "How could anyone hurt her?"

"We don't know if anyone did," Sam said, holding his hand out for the phone.

Skeeter looked at Sam and shook his head.

"She was nice to me," he said, handing the phone back. "She's the only one that's nice to me. Her and Boone. She'd bring us both food. Up by the road there. And she'd sit and talk to me. Sometimes she'd read books to me."

Suddenly a realization dawned on Skeeter.

"You don't think that shoe was hers, do you?" he asked.

"We don't know," Sam answered, relieved that Skeeter had caught up to the conversation.

Skeeter shook his head back and forth violently and put his hands over his eyes.

"No. No. No," he repeated over and over.

"She may have just left town," Sam offered. "But we're still trying to figure it all out."

Skeeter knelt again and began to pet Boone, pulling him close.

"Don't trust them people," he mumbled.

Sam knelt to hear better. "Excuse me?"

Skeeter looked at him, his dark eyes staring hard at Sam.

"Don't trust any of them people," he repeated. "They're all liars and hypocrites."

Boone pulled away from Skeeter and bounded off after a sound in the woods, barking as he ran up the creek.

"Damnit," Skeeter said, standing. "Boone, get back here!"

He started after his dog but turned to Sam.

"If something happened to Amy," he said, shaking a finger at Sam. "they know."

Sam had more questions, but it was clear Skeeter was finished talking. He watched as the old man marched through the woods after his dog.

17

Sam attempted to follow Skeeter into the woods, but the old man clearly had mastered the art of evasion. He had slipped out of sight almost immediately and before Sam realized it, he stumbled upon Toby, who was the person next to him in their manhunt. Toby had seen nothing, and Sam told him about his encounter with Skeeter. At the mere mention of Skeeter's name, Toby began to shake his head.

"Miss Polly's right," he said. "There's something off about that old man. Just wandering out here in the woods. I don't know why the sheriff just don't lock him up."

"Maybe because he hasn't broken the law," Sam suggested politely.

But Toby wasn't buying that argument.

"I'm sure he's done something wrong," he said. "He ain't right in the head."

While Sam couldn't argue with Toby about that, he wasn't so sure that Skeeter was capable of murder.

"I'll tell you something, though," Toby said. "This creek is lined with red rock."

Sam really took in the creek for the first time. Toby was right. From what he could tell, it had a red clay bottom and was lined with large hardened red clay stones. Sam reached down to swipe a finger across one, picking up a dark red stain.

After looking for another hour and then meeting back up with Clyde, Sam was empty-handed and exhausted. But he still had more to do. While Clyde had to get back to his usual rounds for the day, Sam still wanted to follow up on Gus's alibi for the night of Amy's disappearance. That's how he ended up sitting at the bar at Diamond's, the establishment where Gus claimed to have been that night.

It was barely six and the bar was fairly empty except for a handful of the faithful who stopped in on their way home from work. Three men held court at one end of the bar. In the back, a middle-aged couple played pool while another man in a Dallas Cowboys baseball cap watched. The bartender was a big guy, but he looked beat down and bored stiff. He had clearly been working all day and still had a long shift in front of him. Sam tossed a ten on the bar top and asked for a Lone Star. He listened to one of the men at the end of the bar insist to anyone who would listen how tacos are an American food invented in St. Louis.

Why are the dumbest people always the ones to share their 'wisdom' the loudest? Sam wondered.

He turned his attention to the bartender.

"You know Gus Booker?" Sam asked.

"Depends," said the bartender. "What'd he get himself into this time?"

"He says he was here the other night. Is that true?"

"Til closing," the bartender quickly replied.

"I haven't told you which night," Sam said.

"Don't matter," said the bartender. "He's here every night until closing. Comes stumbling in around 7 and don't leave until I kick him out. Why are you asking?"

"You hear about his wife? Amy?" Sam asked.

"Why? She shown back up yet?" a woman's voice asked from behind Sam.

Sam turned to see a woman in a T-shirt and jeans so tight they looked as if they had been spray-painted on. She walked up him, her blonde hair falling over her smoky eyes.

"I heard she left Gus," the woman said with a heavy

drawl, leaning next to Sam a little too close. "It'd be the best thing to ever happen to him."

"Cool it, Mandy," the bartender said, handing her a bottle of beer.

"Oh, shut up, Noah. You know it's true," Mandy said. "He's always been too good for her."

She turned to Sam and held her arms out to either side, putting herself on display. "Don't you think he'd be better off with someone like me?"

Sam took a closer look at the woman. Even though she was probably about the same age as Gus – in her late twenties – hard living had begun to take its toll. She tried to hide it with heavy makeup and sexy clothes, but she was beginning to look like a Jenga tower after the first five moves.

"Well, I never met Amy so I can't really say," Sam answered diplomatically.

"You ain't missed nothing," she snarled back. "Why are you asking about Gus?"

"I'm a private investigator looking into his wife's disappearance," Sam said, choosing his words carefully. "And who are you?"

"I am Mandy Lanford," she said proudly. "And if you wanna know where Gus was the night Amy left him, he was right here. With me."

"So, the two of you..." Sam really wanted her to finish the sentence for him.

"Oh, no way," Mandy replied. "I ain't hooking up with a married man. At least not until he promises he's gonna leave her."

She put her mouth around the lip of the beer bottle and leaned it back in an effort to look seductive – but it was having quite the opposite effect.

"We used to date, you know," Mandy offered. "Back in high school. I was homecoming queen, and he was my king."

Talk about a kingdom falling from grace, Sam thought

"We were gonna get married. Have the prettiest babies in East Texas. And then that Amy witch did something to trap him. But he regretted it. He told me so."

"Mandy, don't go putting words into Gus's mouth," Noah the bartender said, clearly aware of how guilty Mandy was making Gus seem.

"She can stay gone, as far as I'm concerned," Mandy said. "She can go off to ruin some other couple's relationship. Let Gus come back to the woman who really knows how to love him right."

Mandy leaned in closer to Sam, her lips inches from his. "Of course, Gus isn't here yet. Maybe you wanna make me a better offer."

"Mandy, damnit!" Noah yelled. "Lay off the poor man. If I had a hose back here, I'd spray you down."

Mandy giggled and gave Sam a flirtatious wink.

"We were just having a little fun, weren't we?"

Sam nodded. "I think I've had all the fun I can take for one night," he said. "Nice meeting you, Mandy. You behave yourself."

"Never," she said, licking her lips.

He nodded to Noah. "Get a spray bottle filled with cold water," he said. "That'll keep her off the furniture."

18

SAM RETURNED to his motel room, dragging all his fishing gear back inside with him. Except this time, he did it without the false hope that he'd be using it the next day. His mind was jumbled with all the events of the day. All the probabilities. All the potential outcomes. And all the potential suspects.

He laughed to himself, realizing he was collecting suspects for a crime that may not have even been committed. Hell, he wasn't even sure what the crime was. Before he knew what he was doing, he had called his wife.

"Please tell me you're calling from the fishing cabin," Carla said as soon as she answered.

"Looks like the fish'll have to wait another year for me," Sam sighed. "I'm still in Burdett County."

He filled Carla in on the day. Just saying it out loud helped him to make better sense of it all.

"Everyone I meet is acting cagey," he said. "I don't know if it's because they can't fathom a murder could have happened in their corner of the world, or if they're hiding it."

"Trust me, if they watch the news on TV or read the paper at all, they are fully expecting a murder to happen in their neighborhood."

"Then why is the sheriff so convinced nothing happened to Amy? And almost everyone else I talk to is just as sure she's run away from a bad marriage and is never coming back. And from what I've learned, that not only doesn't seem like something Amy would do, but everyone would know that about her."

"So why are they in denial?" Carla asked.

"That's the million-dollar question. At least I've got the county constable helping me out, but he can only do so much. The sheriff keeps freezing him out."

"Why? You'd think he'd welcome the help."

"There's some weird politics going on down here between Miss Polly and the Sheriff and Clyde," Sam answered, rubbing his eyes. "There are a few more people I need to talk to in the morning, including Judy Duncan."

"Amy's sister?"

"Hopefully, she can fill in some gaps."

"About Judy," Carla said in a tone that meant something bad was coming. "Her check bounced."

Sam shook his head. "Of course it did."

"Ask her about it," Carla suggested.

"You know I hate the whole money side of this," Sam groaned. "That's what you're for."

"A, I am for much more than a bookkeeper, Sam Lawson. And B, you should have thought about that when you quit the force to start your own business. Now, man up and ask her about it. But be gentle. Mention it casually. Be subtle."

"You realize subtlety is not my strong point," Sam replied.

"I believe in you," Carla said. "What else is on the docket tomorrow?"

"Talking to a few more people. Shaking down Judy. I may go back to Cypress Meadows to talk to a few more people. And I need to talk to Miss Polly again. Alone. She has her hands in everything, and people like that know everyone's business. Maybe she won't share it in public, but I'm guessing she knows more than she's telling. It's just..."

"Just what?" Carla asked.

Sam's reply dripped with embarrassment and shame. "I'm kind of afraid of her."

19
——————

THE NEXT MORNING, Sam returned to his favorite (and only) diner in the area — this time for an unrushed breakfast, and coffee in a mug instead of a paper cup.

"I'd like two eggs over easy with a side of bacon and sausage," he said to the middle-aged waitress wearing a blue shirt with the name Dixie embroidered above the left chest pocket.

"Hash browns or grits," Dixie asked in a monotone voice.

"Hash browns," Sam replied. "And white toast."

The waitress almost started to ask what type of toast he wanted before realizing he had already answered the question. She nodded and scribbled it all down on an order pad then walked away.

Sam leaned back and scanned the restaurant. It was

seven o'clock on a weekday and the place was packed with what Sam had to assume were regulars. Mostly blue-collar workers grabbing some food before heading to work. A few elderly couples. And a group of five young men and women that looked like they were going to work at a bank. Or possibly the county courthouse. Sam tried to eavesdrop on their conversation, but everyone was mumbling about the day ahead or the night before. Nothing of interest.

It wasn't long before Dixie slid a hot plate in front of Sam. "Here you go, hon," she said. "Can I get you anything else?"

Sam shook his head. "This looks fantastic. Thank you."

Dixie nodded but didn't walk away. She just stared down at Sam. Confused, he took a bite and nodded. "Yep. It's all great. Thank you."

"You're that fella that's looking into Amy Booker leaving town," she said.

Sam looked up at her, wondering if there was more to the statement. He was half disappointed that his morning breakfast retreat was being interrupted by work, but also half curious about what she'd say next.

"I am," Sam said. "You know Amy?"

Dixie nodded. "She came in here every morning like clockwork," the waitress said. "Ordered two coffees and a couple of cinnamon rolls to go."

"The last morning she came in… did she seem odd or different or anything?"

Dixie shook her head. "Same ol' chipper Amy. She'd come clipping in here with a big ol' smile on her face."

She walked away without saying another word and tended to another customer. Sam seized the opportunity to enjoy what he could of his breakfast before, as he feared, she returned.

"I heard y'all found a bloody shoe down by the creek," she said.

"We don't know if it's blood," Sam said. "Could be stains from the red clay. Sheriff's getting some tests run on it."

"You working with the sheriff on this?" Dixie asked.

Sam was surprised at the level of her interrogation.

"He's mainly busy with other things," Sam said diplomatically, not knowing where the waitress's allegiances lay. "I've mainly been working with Constable Harlan."

"Clyde?" Dixie said with a smile. "I guess that makes sense."

Sam was afraid to ask but he knew he had to. "Why do you say it like that?"

"He's been obsessed with that girl since he was a kid," she said.

"Yeah. I heard they were good friends before she started dating Gus."

"They were. Poor Clyde."

"You saying he wanted to be more than friends?" Sam asked.

"Hell, that boy had a crush on her since middle school," Dixie chuckled. "But she never saw it. Or she was good at ignoring it."

"He was always just a friend to her?"

"I remember seeing the two of them almost every day after school. They'd slide into one of the booths right over there," she said, pointing to a row of blue, padded booths along the far wall. "They'd do their homework together and he'd be looking at her all doe eyed. I felt sorry for the kid."

She left for a second and returned with a pot of coffee, topping off Sam's cup without asking.

"Once she started dating Gus, she spent all her time with him. You know how young love is. Poor Clyde would still come back here every day, big ol' pout on his face, and do his homework alone."

"Poor guy," Sam said.

"Yeah, he never got over that," Dixie said. "I think he felt betrayed. Before long, he was avoiding her as much as she was ignoring him. Over the years, it just festered, I guess. I don't know if they ever talked again, but they certainly never made up."

Sam thought about what the waitress was saying.

"Was he ever angry toward her?" Sam asked.

Dixie laughed. "Not to her face," she said. "But you'd see his face sour up if her name was mentioned."

This breakfast was more enlightening than Sam had expected. Could Clyde have resented Amy so much that it had come to a head? Was he working closely with Sam to make sure he stayed off course? Or had his resentment turned into regret? He'd seen it too many times. People fed their resentment or anger toward someone way past the expiration date, thinking that some day down the road, they'd finally make peace with them. But sometimes, 'some day down the road would' hit a dead end, and the opportunity to forgive would be gone forever. Instead, they'd have the regret of words unsaid that would haunt them for the rest of their life.

Regardless, Clyde was not the caring friend he had painted himself to be. And that, unfortunately, put him in the possible suspect category.

20

As soon as Sam arrived at Judy Duncan's small house, he realized the sheriff had not been exaggerating about her. Amy's older sister lived at the dead end of a lower middle-class street. The unmowed grass stood about six inches high but everything else about the front yard seemed meticulously cared for. Colorful flower beds circled the two trees, and a decorative wheelbarrow was filled with more flowers. And not just the impatiens you'd find in most yards. These were flowers of different sizes and shapes — from towering bright yellow sunflowers to sprawling pink geraniums and just about everything in between.

However, it was the other yard decor that really caught Sam's eyes. The life-size Bigfoot silhouette; alien garden gnomes; garden flags that said "BELIEVER" and

"THE TRUTH IS OUT THERE"; a flying saucer hummingbird feeder. The whole yard looked like something between a thrift-store fever dream and a conspiracy theorist's welcome mat.

Sam walked up the front sidewalk, which was painted to look like the yellow brick road from *The Wizard of Oz,* and knocked on the purple door. Judy, looking perfectly normal in a blue pantsuit, opened the door.

The front yard had only been the tip of the iceberg. While the front hallway seemed fairly normal – other than the three cats that immediately appeared, rubbing against Sam's legs – the living room defied expectations. Sheets of plastic covered the walls. And cheap plastic tablecloths covered the couch and recliner, held into place with gray duct tape. It looked like the room was either under construction or a serial killer's kill room.

But the plastic was only the beginning. Aluminum foil covered all the lamp shades. And a multitude of mobiles hung from the ceiling. Mobiles of planets, mobiles of crystals, mobiles of cats. If it could hang from a mobile, it was hanging from Judy's living room ceiling.

And then there was the wall art. Squares and rectangles of aluminum foil hung from the walls as if they were framed photographs. Scattered among these reflective squares were a few actual photographs – they looked to be old family photos, including a large one of two young girls outside the Houston Space Station. Sam instantly recognized the two girls as younger versions of Judy and Amy.

"I know. You must think I'm a loon," Judy said. "Trust me. I'm very aware of what this all looks like. But it's, unfortunately, a necessary evil. The aluminum foil throws off any radio waves or electromagnetic signals in case I'm being bugged or monitored."

Sam nodded, beginning to think the aluminum foil was probably the least crazy thing in the room.

"Please tell me you have good news," she said, motioning for Sam to sit on the plastic-covered couch as she sat down in the recliner. Sam sat down carefully, the plastic squeaking and creaking beneath him.

"The plastic keeps the cats off the furniture," Judy explained.

On cue, a few more cats entered the room, curious about their new visitor. Sam counted six. So far.

"How many cats do you have?" Sam asked politely.

"I think I have eight. Or nine," Judy said. "They come and go. And I think a couple of them may be aliens that have taken feline form, as they do."

Sam nodded like it was common knowledge. One of the cats hopped up in his lap and Sam stroked its long orange and white fur without even thinking about it.

"Is this one an alien?" he asked. "Can you tell?"

"Look at his eyes."

Sam lifted the cat's head up and stared into the cat's hazel eyes.

"Looks pretty normal to me," Sam said.

"That's because he's Emmet," Judy explained. "He's an earthling."

"So, just a cat," Sam confirmed.

Judy smiled. "There's no such thing as 'just a cat'. They're all special creatures. But no. Emmett is not an alien. This other guy however…"

She motioned at another orange and white cat that lazily walked into the room and climbed up on the couch, completely ignoring the plastic lining meant to keep it down. The first thing Sam noticed was its eyes.

"I've never seen eyes this color," Sam said.

"Exactly," Judy replied. "I call him Yams. Because his eyes look like sweet potatoes. He seems to like it, although I'm sure his people call him something very different."

"So, Yams is an alien?" Sam asked.

Yams answered with a dismissive meow and Emmet stepped off Sam's lap. It was as if both cats had grown tired of the conversation at the same time. Sam decided he needed to veer things back to the subject at hand, before he was abducted into some sort of intergalactic feline cult.

"I'll be honest, Judy. I don't have any new news. But I do have a lot of questions."

"So, you know something's not right, right?" Judy asked.

Sam nodded. "I'm not saying anything bad has necessarily happened to your sister, but I get the feeling there's more to the story than she just decided to leave town for a few days."

Judy's eyes lit up. "So, you think she's been abducted?"

Sam held out his hands to calm her down. "Let's not get ahead of ourselves. But things definitely are not adding up."

Judy nodded, trying to contain her excitement. "Do you think they'll return her? Sometimes, they do right away, but other times they could keep her for years."

Sam kicked himself for not noticing the crazy in her eyes when they had first met. But, working in rural East Texas, he had dealt with his share of conspiracy theorists, and he knew the best way to talk to them was to not argue with them.

"All of those things are out of our hands," Sam said. "Unless you can talk to Yams here. But in the meantime, I need to rule out all other possibilities. Just so we can narrow our search for where they may return her."

Judy nodded. "Of course. That makes perfect sense."

"I need to get to know the people in town. Can you help me out?"

Judy nodded again, her emotions bouncing back and forth between relief that Sam believed her and worry about where her sister could actually be.

"What can you tell me about Constable Harlan?" Sam asked.

"Clyde?" The name of a real person brought Judy back to earth, so to speak. She thought for a second as she re-oriented herself. "Poor kid had it bad for my sister back in high school. Not that Amy was completely innocent. She handled things badly. But she was just a kid."

"You're talking about when she started dating Gus?" Sam asked.

"Gus hated Clyde," Judy said. "He was clearly jealous of Amy's relationship with him. Plus, Clyde was smart. Like Amy. Gus was never gonna be able to compete in that category."

"So, what did Amy see in Gus?" Sam asked.

Judy cracked a weak smile. "I can't tell you how many times I asked that same question. To her face, even."

When Judy didn't automatically offer more, Sam pushed the conversation. "And?"

"She never gave me an answer," Judy said. "I don't think she knew. And I think she definitely regretted it.

But Amy was the shy little bookworm. She didn't have a lot of friends and never had a boyfriend. I think when the high school quarterback started paying attention to her, it made her feel special. I think she was seduced by that."

"So, Gus was the All-American football hero. Her Prince Charming."

Judy laughed. "Oh, God, no. He was a good football player, but he was no Prince Charming. He was trouble back then. I think that bad boy thing appealed to her. Amy was as straight an arrow as there could be."

"The ol' Sandy and Danny syndrome," Sam said with a nod.

Judy's eyebrows furrowed in confusion and then she brightened up. "Oh! From Grease! Right. I always hated that she gave up her morals to get her guy. My sister's life is proof of how that really turns out."

Sam smiled. "Yeah, it's amazing what a pair of tight leather pants can do to your personality. Danny clearly won that round. I guess it made for a better song, though."

I'm talking about Grease in a crazy cat lady's plastic-covered living room, he thought.

"What about Amy's job?" Sam asked, yanking his tone back to something more professional. "Her boss said she was working on some sort of history side project there. You know anything about that?"

Judy smiled. "She was always digging up some history tidbits. She loved that stuff."

"She ever tell you about anything she found that could be criminal? Something that someone wouldn't want discovered?" Sam asked.

Judy chewed her bottom lip as she thought for a moment. "No," she said, shaking her head. "Nothing. But we never talked about any of that stuff, so it doesn't mean she hadn't."

She leaned forward. "Do you think she found out something that got her in trouble? Maybe she found proof of alien life."

Sam shook his head. "I'm looking for anything at this point," he shrugged. "I don't know what she had found. Or if she even found anything. I'm just thinking out loud."

They sat in silence for a few seconds. Sam could tell Judy wanted to say something and he was willing to wait as she built up her courage.

"I heard about the shoe," she finally said, there was a tremble in her voice and she began wringing her hands nervously. "Do you think it's hers?"

Sam let out a sigh. He had hoped that news hadn't made its way back to the sister.

"I honestly don't know," Sam said. "But the sheriff sent it out to see if there's a DNA sample. If it's any consolation, he doesn't think it's your sister's. Neither does Miss Polly."

Judy stiffened. "Miss Polly?"

Sam nodded. "She's very concerned about your sister," he added.

Judy nodded. Talking about the shoe had shifted the mood in the room and Judy spoke more softly. "Miss Polly practically took us in after Mama died. I can be a handful, I admit it. And me and Amy were both a bit adrift there. And Gus wasn't any help, as you can imagine. But Miss Polly would show up with a casserole to make sure I was eating. She'd take one to Amy, too. She somehow got Gus to be more understanding. And when Amy wanted to get a job, Miss Polly helped her."

"She really took care of the two of you," Sam said, half surprised.

Judy nodded, forcing a smile. "She's that way with everyone. She'll just take care of you, without question or judgment."

"An old softie, huh?"

"Oh, she's not soft," Judy said. "She expects you to pull your own weight. She'll happily help someone that's willing to help themselves, but she's got no patience for freeloaders. Or people that do her people wrong."

Judy's mood began to lighten as she chuckled at a memory. "One time, Luella James saw Miss Polly at the grocery store. She was all bruised up from her husband. Then Leo, her husband, came in to get Luella, and Miss Polly started storming toward him. She snatched a push broom out of this guy's hands and, without missing a beat, she broke the handle off over her knee. Snapped it right in half and never stopped walking. She swung that stick like a baseball bat and hit Leo square in the jaw. He fell to the floor like a rag doll, but she kept right on hitting him. Leo's a big man but he started scrambling and crawling away from her and took off out of that grocery store with his tail tucked between his legs."

Judy raised her right hand. "I swear to God it happened. I was standing right over by the corn and saw the whole thing. And then she took in Luella. Put her up in an empty trailer home she had, got her all set up. And hired a lawyer for her so she could divorce that piece of trash. That's the kind of person Miss Polly is."

"I'll be sure to stay on her good side," Sam said.

"If you're helping find Amy, you already are," Judy replied.

21

____

THE SUN WAS CREEPING HIGHER in the sky, and the temperatures were already in the low 90s. The still, humid air stuck to Sam's sweaty skin as he walked through the back end of Cypress Meadows. He'd returned to finish up what he'd started. There were still a few residents he hadn't spoken to, but first, he wanted to walk through the rest of the area near the creek.

Dragonflies buzzed his head on their own exploratory missions. Sam swatted the air to keep them — and the swarms of mosquitos — at bay. He walked through the tall grass, hoping to see something the search party didn't find. He knew it was pretty much a fool's errand, but something in his gut insisted he give the area a second look. And with not much else to go on, his gut was calling more and more of the shots.

At first, he had seen the shoe as a major breakthrough. But it was already bringing up new questions. First off, why was her shoe found by the creek? Had she been there and lost it, or had she been taken by someone, and they had been getting rid of evidence? What about the other shoe? Or, God forbid, Amy?

So, why am I sweating my ass off out here? Sam wondered.

Because his gut was telling him to. And either his gut was on to something, or it loved torturing its owner.

Up ahead he saw movement, as a figure walked out of the tree line. The figure seemed to notice Sam at the same time, and both men froze. Sam recognized him. It was Toby Clague, the man he had put in charge of the search the day before.

What's he doing out here again? Sam wondered.

Toby started walking toward Sam.

He was a big man, probably in his fifties. About six feet tall, in good shape, and had short salt and pepper hair that was thinning on top.

"Looks like we both had the same idea," Toby said with a smile as he trudged closer.

"Looks that way," Sam said, sizing up Toby. He seemed jittery and his eyes darted back and forth behind Sam, as if he was making sure they were alone. Still, he was smiling and honestly seemed a bit relieved to see Sam. But the way he had walked out of the woods set off a faint alarm in Sam's mind. He made a mental note of the location where he had emerged.

"You're not gonna find anything out here," Toby said. "I've been up since the crack of dawn scouring the fields. I even got my metal detector out. Used it until the battery died. Then I started going through the woods a bit."

"You're pretty committed to this," Sam said.

Toby wiped the sweat off his forehead. "You got kids?"

Sam nodded but offered nothing more.

"I got a daughter," Toby continued. "Not much younger than Amy Booker. I can't imagine what I'd do if something happened to her. And honestly, you and the constable are about the only other people that seemed concerned."

"Do you think something bad happened to her?" Sam asked.

Toby shrugged. "I'd rather play it safe than sorry. That's what we're doing. Right?"

Sam nodded.

"I gotta cool off and get something to drink," Toby said. "You want anything? Water? Iced tea?"

Sam felt a wave of relief. He was itching to check out the woods where Toby had emerged.

"Nah, you go ahead," Sam said. "I just got started out here, so I'll look a little longer."

Toby studied him. He hesitated for a second, as if he was deciding whether or not he should leave Sam alone. Finally, he spoke.

"Save yourself the trouble of looking back there," he said, pointing to the portion of the woods where he had emerged. "I've combed every inch. I'd look over that way."

As Sam expected, he pointed to a part of the woods in the opposite direction.

"I checked there yesterday," Sam said, looking closely at Toby to see if he flinched in any way. But the man simply nodded and grinned.

"Well, it gets all cut off from the road back there," Toby said. "The creek goes through a big viaduct to the other side then continues on another mile or so. If you wanna wait, I won't be long."

Sam smiled. "Nah, you go on. There's still a lot of area to check and I gotta be somewhere in an hour."

It was a lie, but Sam wanted to plant the seed that he would be missed if something happened to him. Just in case.

Toby nodded and smiled. Sam's gut twisted. Something about him was giving Sam the creeps.

Toby wished Sam luck and walked back toward his

small, gray house. Sam immediately headed for the woods. He started toward the area Toby had suggested, but as soon as he disappeared into the tree line, he switched course and headed to the area where Toby had been.

22

———————

MAYBE HE WAS BEING paranoid and overreacting, but Sam trusted his gut. And his gut was telling him something was wrong. He trudged through the woods, looking back to make sure Toby hadn't decided to come after him.

The air smelled of damp earth, old leaves, and that sharp iron tang from the red clay. Sam could hear the creek flowing to his right, which he used to help keep his bearings. There was no trail to follow, and the thick woods were filled with pine trees, cypress and wild brush. And everything looked the same.

When he reached the area where Toby had been, he slowed down, scanning the woods carefully. Looking for anything out of the ordinary. He turned and started walking toward the sound of the creek, his eyes moving back and forth across the russet carpet of pine needles and old cypress bark. He looked up for snags of fabric stuck on a tree branch or trunk. He checked the ground for patches of dried blood.

Dry twigs cracked under his boots as he slowly trudged forward. Ahead, he could see bright patches of white light dancing through the trees from the sun reflecting off of water. The trees began to thin as he neared the creek. It was about twenty yards to the other side and appeared deep. At least, too deep to walk across without getting soaked. Sam remembered Toby's clothes had not been wet, so he clearly hadn't crossed it either.

Then he heard something further up the creek. It was an irregular knocking and rustling sound that Sam immediately imagined could be the sound of someone trying to break free from something.

He began to walk quickly in the direction of the sound, following the creek and looking ahead for any motion. The creek took a sharp turn to the left and disappeared into the woods. Sam stayed the course, unsure of what he would find when he rounded the curve.

The sound grew louder. He knew he was getting close. He was regretting leaving his gun in his truck, so he grabbed a thick branch about the size of a baseball bat.

Up ahead, just far enough into the woods to not be completely seen, something was moving. Sam saw glimpses of red and yellow. Enough for him to know it wasn't an animal. He began to creep toward the colors. It was clearly a person. They were moving back and forth between two spots about five feet apart from each other.

Sam stepped into the woods and a loud branch cracked under his boot. He froze. The person in the woods spun around to look at Sam, but Sam still couldn't see enough to identify them. Then the person crouched, as if to hide.

"I can see you," Sam yelled.

The person stayed crouched, and Sam moved cautiously toward them.

"You might as well show yourself," Sam said, close enough he no longer needed to yell.

He tightened the grip on his stick and held it over a shoulder, like a batter ready to take a fastball. He crept closer, ready to swing, until he got close enough to see the person.

"Skeeter," he said in a loud sigh, loosening the grip on the stick and dropping it to his side. He wasn't sure if he was relieved or disappointed.

Skeeter stiffened like a cornered raccoon, his shoulders hunched and his eyes wide beneath his heavy, wiry brows.

"Leave me alone," Skeeter said.

Skeeter was pulling tattered clothes out of one black plastic trash bag and shoving other things in a different trash bag. His hands moved quickly, like someone running out of time.

"Sorry," Sam said. "I didn't mean to creep up on you."

He looked around, noticing a tattered blue tarp draped over a low branch that jutted out of a tree to form a makeshift tent. Empty plastic jugs and cans were littered around a black ash circle, the remnants of a campfire. The air smelled like old smoke, wet earth and the musk of someone who'd lived outdoors for too long.

"What are you doing, Skeeter?" Sam asked.

"That ain't none of your damn business," Skeeter snapped back.

"Looks like you're packing up," Sam said.

Skeeter kept loading up one bag and emptying the other, muttering to himself under his breath.

"I was back out here looking for Amy Booker again," Sam said, still attempting to make conversation.

Skeeter immediately softened. "Amy's a good girl. She likes fishing, too. We talked about fishing. Sunfish mainly. Bass."

"When did you talk about it?" Sam asked.

"In my dreams," he said matter-of-factly. "Good things happen in Skeeter's dreams. Not like out here."

"What happens out here?" Sam asked, trying to keep up with Skeeter's wandering mind.

"Is that what that other fella was doing, too?" Skeeter asked.

"Doing what?"

"Looking for Amy."

Sam had to assume he meant Toby.

"I think so," Sam said. "Did you see him? Was he doing anything?"

Skeeter looked at Sam like he was crazy.

"It ain't my business. When I saw him, I just went the other way."

"Are you packing your stuff?" Sam asked. "You leaving?"

"Too many people around here," Skeeter said. "If I stay, they'll come after Skeeter."

Sam was thrown off by the choice of words.

"What do you mean come after you? Why would they come after you?"

Skeeter studied Sam's face. His nostrils flared slightly, and his fingers tightened around the edges of the garbage bags. He gave Sam a knowing look and then started throwing more of the clothes in the trash bags.

"You're wasting your time up here," he finally said.

"What do you mean?" Sam asked.

Skeeter shook his head. "It's all wrong. It's all wrong out here now."

"What's all wrong?" Sam asked.

Skeeter shook his head back and forth, growing more manic. He turned away and yanked the blue tarp tent down in a sudden, almost violent, movement. As he rolled it up, he turned back to Sam.

"You gotta gun?" Skeeter said.

Another curveball of a question.

"I do. It's registered."

"Give it to me," Skeeter said, holding out his hand.

"I'm not gonna give you my gun!" Sam said.

"Give it to me!" Skeeter yelled angrily.

"Skeeter, I'm not gonna give you my gun," Sam said calmly. "I don't have it on me right now anyway."

Skeeter stared at Sam. Sam couldn't tell if he saw anger or fear in his eyes.

"Why do you need my gun?" Sam asked.

"Protection!" Skeeter shouted.

"Protection from who?"

Skeeter looked around wide-eyed, as if he saw something. But the way his eyes darted around the trees, Sam figured he had to be hallucinating. The man's entire body was trembling in nervous energy.

"She was a good girl," Skeeter said. "She didn't deserve it."

"Are you talking about Amy?" Sam asked, trying to keep up. "What do you know?"

Skeeter froze. Then he deflated as the manic energy rushed from his body. He looked up at Sam, more relaxed and acting as if nothing had happened or nothing had been said.

"It's not safe out here," he said.

He threw a few more things in a trash bag and then pulled both bags over his shoulder. They looked impossibly heavy, but Skeeter braced his thin frame and somehow managed to bear their weight.

"I gotta find Boone."

23

———

SKEETER MADE it clear he had nothing else to say as he slowly headed up the creek with his heavy load. Sam thought about following him. He couldn't tell if the old man was angry or frightened or both. Either way, he seemed to know something he wasn't telling, and Sam knew a man like Skeeter wasn't going to share anything until he was ready.

But Sam thought it was more than a coincidence that Skeeter was getting the hell out of Dodge right after Toby had been in the same area. Had Toby said something to scare him? Accused him? Threatened him?

As those questions tumbled through Sam's head, he sifted through the rubble Skeeter had left behind. After ten minutes or so, satisfied there was nothing that could help him find Amy, Sam decided he needed to go to the source. He turned and headed back toward Toby's house.

He hadn't walked far when he heard someone walking through the trees next to him. Sounds had a way of echoing in the woods and Sam felt like it was coming from his left. He turned and peered into the dense woods, looking for movement between the trees. When he heard a branch crack loudly behind him, he spun around.

Toby was walking toward him quickly, a frustrated look on his face.

"I told you I already checked this part of the woods," he said.

Sam noticed a hint of nervousness in Toby's clipped tone. There was a tightness in his jaw and a twitch at the corner of his eye.

"I was just working my way back up the creek," Sam said calmly. "Never hurts to double check an area. You're welcome to double check where I started."

Toby reached Sam and looked around, visibly worried.

"Did you see Skeeter?" Toby asked.

"Did you see him when you were out here?" Sam asked back.

Toby sized up Sam, carefully calculating his reply.

"I did," he finally answered. "Up by the creek."

"Did you talk to him?" Sam asked.

"Did you?" Toby asked back. "You didn't spook him, did you?"

He looked back toward the creek. "You gotta be careful with that old fool," Toby said. "You say the wrong thing; he'll disappear for weeks."

Part of Sam felt embarrassed that he had potentially said the wrong thing, but he kept his poker face, admitting to nothing.

"Did you say anything to him?" Sam asked. "He seemed pretty spooked."

Toby looked back to the creek again. He was growing more and more nervous.

"Is he still there?" Toby asked. "He didn't leave, did he?"

Sam nodded. "I'm afraid I caught him mid-flight."

"And you didn't stop him?" Toby asked.

"I couldn't make him do anything," Sam said. "I'm a private eye, not a cop. I don't have that kind of jurisdiction."

"Damnit!" Toby yelled as he began to pace back and forth. He stopped and pointed toward Skeeter's campground. "If something bad happened to Amy, he's responsible. I guarantee you."

"He's now the second person I've received a guarantee of their guilt," Sam said. "Why him? What makes you so sure? And how are you so sure something even happened to Amy?"

Toby looked at Sam as if he had asked why one plus one doesn't equal five.

"I don't trust him," Toby said. "No one does. Living out here in the woods. Going through people's trash. God knows what kind of a creep he is."

"All I can tell for sure is he's homeless and he keeps to himself," Sam said.

"Oh, he's not homeless," Toby replied. "He's got an old farmhouse right outside of town."

Sam was shocked by that bit of news.

"So, he's just a big outdoorsman?" Sam asked, half sarcastically.

"About fifteen years ago, his wife and kid died in a car accident," Toby said. "Skeeter went off the deep end. Didn't leave his house forever. The way I heard it is the sheriff went to check on him and found the man living in complete squalor. Trash everywhere. It stunk to high heaven. But Skeeter wouldn't leave. The sheriff left and came back with some county folks from Protective Services but this time, the house was empty. No one saw him at all for a long time. Then he started showing up in the woods. He's been out here ever since."

"No shit," Sam replied, shocked.

Toby shook his head. "He ain't right in the head," Toby said. "But the sheriff says he can't do nothing.

There's got to be some trespassing laws or sleeping overnight on state property laws or something. But if there is, the sheriff ain't enforcing 'em. And now a poor girl is paying the price for it."

That would explain the sheriff's state of denial about Amy's disappearance, Sam thought. If something has happened to Amy and Skeeter were involved, the sheriff would have to feel guilty. What's more, his constituents would see Amy's death as his fault.

"I've gotta ask you a question," Sam said. "So I can keep you out of this. Where you were between 9pm and 7am the night Amy went missing?"

Toby's jaw dropped and his face reddened. "What the hell? You think I'm guilty?"

Sam shook his head, softening his tone to lower Toby's defenses. "Not at all. I was wondering where you were in case you had heard or seen something."

Toby nodded, buying Sam's imaginary motive, but clearly still on guard. "I was at home. I watched TV then went to bed. I was up at 6 and on my way to work by 7."

"And you didn't see or hear anything unusual?"

Toby shook his head. "Not that I remember. But these trees act as a buffer from a lot of noises by the creek."

"I imagine. But surely, you'd hear something like a scream."

Toby seemed to think hard about his response.

"Possibly," he said slowly. "I've never heard a scream from down here, so I couldn't say for sure."

"It's a shame. That would sure help pin it on Skeeter," Sam said, offering easy bait to Toby.

He could see Toby regretting his answer. If he was trying to make Skeeter the scapegoat, he had just messed up an easy way to do it.

"I sleep like a tank," Toby said. "Hell, a fox could be screaming in my living room, and I wouldn't hear it. Did you ask any of my neighbors?"

"I haven't," Sam lied.

In truth, he had asked that very question of Toby's neighbors the day before and no one had seen or heard anything. But he didn't feel like Toby needed to know that. Guilty people make stupid mistakes when they get nervous. If Toby was guilty of anything, he'd most likely show his cards soon enough.

"You need to put your focus on Skeeter," Toby said, shifting the conversation. "He's acting real suspicious lately. Hanging around here yesterday while y'all were talking to people. And he's always looked at girls in a creepy way. I wouldn't let my daughter near these woods when she was little. Plus, he knows these woods better than anyone."

Sam had to admit that many signs did point toward the eccentric old man in the woods. But Toby's insistence on Skeeter being guilty of a crime no one was sure had even been committed pointed a few fingers back at him.

He wanted to check Toby's house, but knew the man was not going to make that easy. He'd need Clyde to get a warrant for that. In the meantime, he needed to pay a visit to Skeeter's abandoned home.

Unfortunately, there were some other people interested in that house.

24

On the outskirts of Elsip, a Ford Bronco lurched slowly up an overrun dirt road. Between giant potholes to huge mounds of grass, the drive was almost enough to make the three teenagers carsick. The Bronco drove slowly up the road, passing an empty field to the left and a barbed wire fence line to the right. On the other side of the fence, a small herd of cows munched on Bermuda grass and watched the Bronco with bored curiosity.

The two-story farmhouse sat at the top of a hill, its black tile roof overrun with moss and thick strands of Virginia Creeper climbing up the sides of the home.

Skeeter Wells' old home.

Most of the windows were missing glass panes, and

the ones that were still attached to the frames were shattered. The teenagers parked the Bronco and they all climbed out.

"I've never been here in the middle of the day," Taylor, a lanky, sixteen-year-old said, staring at the building.

"Trust me. It's way better than coming at night," Aaron replied, slapping Taylor on the shoulder and wiping his wavy blonde hair out of his eyes.

The third teen, Colton, opened the tailgate of the Bronco and grabbed a bag.

"Let's just get the stuff and go," he said. "This place gives me the creeps. I don't care if it's daylight."

Taylor and Aaron teased their friend, who remained focused on the task at hand.

"It better still be here," he said.

"Calm down," Aaron said, skipping up the creaky gray steps to the old house. "Nobody comes out here."

"What about the old man?" Taylor asked, following his friend.

"Crazy Man Skeeter?" Aaron said. "Nah. He's not been back to this place in decades."

Living at home with limited privacy, the teens had been using Skeeter's old home as a place to stash beer and marijuana. Today, they were making a run to pick up their "supplies" for a pasture party that night.

Colton stopped before walking up the steps, his eyes

fixed on the sagging house like it might look back at him.

"Come on!" Aaron said. "Haven't you ever been in a haunted house before?"

Not wanting to appear scared, Colton shot a middle finger at Aaron and walked up behind him, being careful not to fall through any decayed wood.

The old Wells home definitely looked like a haunted house, certainly nothing like the happy family home it had been decades earlier, before tragedy hollowed it out as fast as it did its owner. Skeeter lost his family and then his mind. And the house had collapsed right along with him.

The front door dangled on a single hinge and the teens pulled it aside to enter. The inside was dark, damp and dusty. An overwhelming stench of mildew made their eyes immediately water. Colton turned on the flashlight and swept it across the living room. Most of the belongings, including the furniture, had long been removed by scrappers and junk collectors. Graffiti now covered the walls – mostly crude drawings, name calling, and a few predictable pentagrams spray-painted by teenagers hoping to start urban legends about devil worship.

Taylor listened for any suspicious sounds, but other than their own footsteps, the only other noise was from the occasional rodent scurrying out of sight.

Without speaking, the three boys moved to the kitchen. Colton turned the flashlight off; enough sunlight leaked through the broken windows for them to see – what little there was to see, that is. Like the other rooms, this one had been picked clean. One broken chair leaned in a corner, and the electric oven and refrigerator had been pulled away from the wall, as if someone began to take them but decided they were too heavy to bother with.

Aaron noticed something on the floor behind the fridge. A small photograph lay half-buried in dust.

"Check this out," he said, holding it out for Taylor. The yellowed photo showed a happily family of three – a smiling husband and wife and their daughter, who looked to be about eight.

"You think that's the family?" Taylor asked. "Is that guy Crazy Man Skeeter?"

The man in the photo was much younger than the old man in the woods, but his deep-set, dark eyes were unmistakable.

"Guys," Colton whispered loudly.

Aaron and Taylor turned around to see Colton in the hallway, motioning urgently.

They followed him down a hall, where Colton was pointing to a half-open door.

"What the hell?" Aaron said. "Did you forget to shut it last time?"

"Don't blame me. I always shut it," Colton said.

"You think someone's been here?" Taylor said. "You think they're here now?"

"Nobody is here now," Colton said. "But someone clearly was."

The three teens opened the door and looked inside. Colton shone the flashlight beam down the steep wooden stairs.

"Anybody here?" Taylor yelled as they began their slow descent into the basement.

Most homes in East Texas didn't have basements. The red clay base was too hard to dig through. But some homes were lucky enough to be built on pockets of softer soil. This must have been one of them.

As they walked down the stairs they were all overwhelmed by a dank stench that made their stomach turn. The room was small, and they could see most of it from the stairs. However, a large shelf had been pulled out into the center of the room. It was filled with boxes, blocking the view of whatever was on the other side.

"Someone's been down here, man," Taylor said. "That wasn't there."

"Let's get our stash and get out of here," Colton said.

The problem was that their stash was on the other side of the shelf.

Feeling rightfully spooked, they crept slowly toward it, not knowing what they would find on the other side.

Aaron turned the corner first and stumbled back in horror as Taylor and Colton rounded the corner. They all froze in shock, staring at the body of a barefoot woman hanging from a rope.

25

THE NEXT DAY, Sam sat in his truck outside the sheriff's office, talking to Clyde on speaker phone

"I swear. I searched through the entire house. It was the same morning you came to town," Clyde said. "Top to bottom."

"And you checked the basement?" Sam said.

"Of course. I looked down the stairs," Clyde replied. "I would have seen a body hanging there."

"Those teenagers said the body was hidden behind a shelf," Sam argued. "Did you go all the way down into the basement or just look down the stairs?"

"I walked halfway down the stairs," Clyde said defensively. "But there was no shelf blocking my view. I could see the entire basement, and I'm telling you, Amy was not there."

"So, you're saying she showed up there after you had searched?"

"Or someone brought her there," Clyde suggested. "But good luck getting the sheriff to investigate that."

"It does sound like a crazy conspiracy theory," Sam replied, not yet willing to admit that he was leaning toward the same explanation. "What about that Toby guy? Lives in one of those homes by the creek?"

"What about him?" Clyde asked. "Are you adding him to your suspect pool now? Let me save you the trouble. Toby's a little rough around the edges, but he's a good man. A good father."

"Looks – hell, even actions – can be deceiving," Sam countered.

Clyde laughed. "You really do see everyone guilty until proven innocent, don't you?"

"I have been told I have a suspicious mind," Sam said. "But that's the beauty of having my POV. I can see things at face value, without knowing a person's past or reputation. And something about Toby rubbed me the wrong way. Can you get a warrant to search his place?"

"A warrant is gonna have to go through the judge," Clyde said. "And the judge is the sheriff's first cousin. So, until we get the sheriff on board, I wouldn't count on any warrants."

Sam looked up at the sheriff's office in front of him. "Well, let me see what I can do about that."

Sam thumbed through the coroner's preliminary - and obviously rushed - report on Amy Booker. No internal autopsy had been conducted, and no forensics samples were being sent for testing. Yet the coroner seemed confident enough to declare that Amy's cause of death was "asphyxiation due to strangulation by ligature" and the manner of death was suicide.

Granted, there were no other possibly fatal wounds on her body – no gunshot wounds, no knife wounds, no blunt force trauma. At face value, suicide made the most sense. But that was Sam's problem: the coroner had built his conclusion entirely on face-value evidence.

There was one other issue: the coroner estimated the time of death to be five days earlier — about the same time Amy went missing. If Amy had hanged herself then, her body would have had to be in the basement when Clyde searched it.

Sam tried to explain this to the sheriff but was met with a head shake and a chuckle.

"Lord forbid he just admit he didn't do a thorough search," the sheriff said. "If I've got to bet on Clyde's shoddy investigative abilities or my coroner's report, I'm putting my money on R.J. Sanders. He's been our coroner for nearly forty years now. He's served this county well and I trust his opinion."

"They could both be right," Sam suggested.

The sheriff laughed again. "I'm sure you're gonna tell me how that would work."

Sam was quick to answer. "Amy died somewhere else and her body was moved to the abandoned house."

"You watch too much TV."

"We could easily find out, if your coroner conducted a full autopsy," Sam protested.

"You know as well as I do that, sometimes, you just don't need to," the sheriff countered. "When it's so obvious what happened, why would you want to stir the pot like that? It would only serve to hurt a family that's already suffering."

The mention of family made Sam wonder how Amy's sister had taken the news. He asked the sheriff how it went.

"She did not take it well," Sheriff Wheeler said. "Miss Polly is sitting with her now. Poor girl may need to be put on a suicide watch herself."

"So, you really believe Amy died by suicide?" Sam asked.

"It makes sense," the sheriff said. "She was fed up with her life. Nowhere to go. Those boys found her in the basement swinging from a rope over a support beam - a chair kicked aside. No sign of struggle. And no other injuries to the body, except the rope burn around her neck."

It was true. But there were still unanswered questions.

"But why go there? She had no history there," Sam argued.

"That we know of," the sheriff countered. "And she probably went there so no one would bother her. Who knows? She was clearly not in a good state of mind. The poor girl."

"But no suicide note?" Sam countered. "From everything I've learned about her, that doesn't sound like Amy at all. She'd at least have left her sister something. And where's her purse? And her car? How'd she even get out there? The house is in the middle of nowhere."

Sam's constant and stubborn questioning finally wore the sheriff down enough that he relented to getting a group of volunteers to comb the area around Skeeter's home for Amy's purse and car. Sam knew he wasn't going to get anywhere with his other theories without more evidence, so he backed down for now. But he had a plan.

Sam returned to his truck and made a call.

"Hey, there," Carla cooed into the phone. "This is a pleasant surprise."

"How busy are you?" Sam blurted out, skipping over

any flirtations or small talk. The urgency in his voice startled her.

"Uhm, it's actually pretty quiet over here," she replied, wincing for the expected 'pretty dead around here' pun Sam had never been able to resist.

"I need you to come down to Burdett," Sam said, not taking his own bait.

"What's going on, Sam?" Carla asked, now slightly worried.

Sam filled her in on the discovery of Amy's body, the rushed coroner's report, and the too-easy suicide theory.

"What did her neck look like?" Carla asked.

"I don't know," Sam said. "I mean, there was a mark from the rope."

"But was it just a rope burn? Or was their bruising? And what about a drool trail? Or petechiae?"

"I don't know what you're saying, but it's kinda turning me on."

Carla ignored Sam's quip "And the coroner didn't do an internal investigation?"

"No," Sam said, taking her cue to be serious. "That's why I need you here. Assist this coroner with the autopsy. A thorough autopsy."

"I can't just show up and demand he conduct a second autopsy," Carla said. "I don't have that kind of jurisdiction."

"You're a chief medical examiner. Don't you outrank him?" Sam asked.

"We're in different counties," Carla reminded him.

They both sat in silence, unsure of their next moves.

"You're in Burdett County," Carla said. "The coroner is an elected position there, right?"

"If you say so," Sam said.

"I'm pretty sure it is," Carla said, talking out loud to herself now. Sam could hear her typing on her computer's keypad. "And it looks like Mr. R.J. Sanders is up for re-election next year."

"You planning on offering to make a campaign donation?" Sam asked.

"No, but I *am* going to suggest it's better to be seen as the guy who brings in an expert when needed, instead of the guy dealing with a negligence lawsuit for not doing so. And I feel pretty confident that's the type of thing I could convince Judy Duncan she needed to do. Unless of course, Mr. Sanders had done everything he could possibly do."

"Why, Carla Lawson, are you going to threaten Mr. Sanders?" Sam smiled.

"I'm going to present him with two options and let him choose the smarter one," Carla said back.

"Did you just go all *Godfather* on me? I'm serious. You're really turning me on," Sam said with a grin.

"Well, save it for later, handsome," she replied. "I

need to make a call to Mr. Sanders, take care of a few things at work, and get packed. I'll be there tomorrow."

As she spoke, Clyde's SUV rolled up beside him. Clyde got out and tapped on Sam's window.

"Just as well," Sam said. "The constable just pulled up."

"Again?" Carla asked. "Should I be jealous?"

Sam chuckled. "Keep me posted on your call with Coroner Clueless."

He hung up as Clyde opened the passenger door and climbed in. "Sam, thank God I found you."

26

ON THE OTHER side of town, Gus slumped over his whiskey, staring into the glass for answers to questions he didn't know how to ask. The bar was dark and mostly empty; the only sound was the lonely Hank Williams song crying like a whippoorwill from the jukebox.

Gus took a deep breath and shut his eyes. Four hours earlier, he'd been sunk into his couch watching reruns of *The Rifleman,* when Sheriff Wheeler showed up at his door to tell him they'd found Amy's body – hanging in the basement of Skeeter Wells' old home.

He tossed back the rest of the whiskey and set the glass back hard on the bar top to get the bartender's attention. Noah walked over and poured more Jack Daniel's into Gus's glass.

"Anything else I can get for you, buddy?" Noah asked quietly.

Gus answered by throwing back the entire glass and tapping the rim.

"You might wanna slow it down a bit," Noah cautioned.

"You might wanna just do your damn job," Gus growled.

Noah nodded. Starting a fight with Gus tonight would've been like poking a gator with a short stick. Best to let him drink himself to a stupor. Gus wasn't an angry drunk, so Noah didn't have to worry about that. Gus's problem was he didn't know when to quit, so he'd drink till he passed out. Noah had lost count of the number of times he'd let Gus sleep it off in the cot he kept in the storage room.

Besides, if a man ever deserved to drink, it was on the day he found out his wife had hung herself.

Noah knew the score with Gus and Amy and their complicated, half-forgotten marriage, and he wasn't about to rewrite it into something that it wasn't. But Amy had still been his wife, and no matter what love was lost through the years, there'd once been enough to bring them together and to keep them together for ten years.

Noah stared at Gus looking into his glass, oblivious to anything and anyone around him. The two men had grown up together. Played football together. Noah had watched Gus slide from Elsip's golden boy football hero to its resident unemployed drunk. Part of him felt guilty for enabling it, but he rationalized that Gus would've just found another bar. At least Noah could keep a watchful eye over his friend here.

He heard the door open and when he looked up, his shoulders sagged in disappointment. There was one thing he'd never been able to protect Gus from: Mandy Lanford. He shot her a glare, letting her know to give Gus his space. Mandy rolled her eyes and slid on to the stool next to the new widower.

"Can I get my usual?" she asked Noah.

Her voice was quiet and subdued. Noah was relieved she was at least reading the room, and he poured a Corona Light from the tap. She took a long swallow, then leaned down, to look up at Gus's face.

"You doing okay there?" she asked quietly.

When she patted his back, Gus stiffened. She pulled her hand away, unsure what to do or say but unwilling to just sit there.

"I know this is a tough time for you," she finally said. "But I want you to know that I am here for you. Whenever you are ready. I am here."

"Mandy, give the man a little breathing room," Noah interjected.

Mandy cut a glare at him then turned her attention back to Gus.

"At least now you know," she continued. "As awful as it is, it's better than having no closure."

She paused, half expecting Gus to respond. But he never looked up from his whiskey. She wasn't even sure if he heard her. But that didn't stop her from pressing on.

"You need to grieve. That's the right thing to do. Out of respect. But then you can start moving on. And I will be here for you. I want you to know that."

Gus stirred at the words. He tipped his head toward her – his face twisted with grief, shock and anger. It settled into a bone-deep exhaustion. He shut his eyes and exhaled slowly through his nostrils, deflating like a worn-out tire. Then he slowly turned his attention back to his glass –not drinking it. Just staring.

"Mandy, why don't we leave Gus to himself for a while," Noah said.

The words were gentle but the look on his face made it clear he wasn't making a suggestion. He moved her drink down the bar and motioned for Mandy to follow.

"I'll be right down there if you need me, baby," Mandy said. "You don't have to go through this alone."

27

CLYDE'S EYES were puffy and bloodshot. He was trying to hide it, but he had clearly been crying. He sat in Sam's truck, staring dead ahead to help control his emotions.

"We both saw this coming," he said. "If the sheriff would have been doing his job from the get-go, we could've saved her."

"You don't know that, Clyde," Sam said. "The coroner said she'd been dead about five days. That's right when she went missing. She was gone before anyone realized she was missing."

"And now they're just writing it off to suicide," Clyde grumbled.

"I'm guessing you don't buy that either," Sam replied.

"Everyone wants to sweep this under the rug," Clyde said. "Pretend like nothing happened. Or at least like nothing sinister happened. But Amy was murdered. As sure as the sun's gonna rise in the morning. And it's up to you and me to get justice for her."

Clyde's eyes started to well up again.

"Why would anyone kill Amy?" he said, fighting the sob building in his throat. "She was an angel. There was no one sweeter on the planet. She did not deserve this."

"I just got off the phone with my wife," Sam said. "She's a medical examiner – one of the best. She's gonna come down tomorrow morning and work with the coroner to conduct a full autopsy."

"I can't imagine R.J. is gonna agree to that."

"R.J.'s not gonna have much of a choice. But you need to be ready for the possibility that she's gonna come back with the same conclusion."

"You know she won't," Clyde said. "That asshole husband of hers killed her and we both know it."

"We do NOT know that," Sam replied, his voice sharp as a snapped twig. "Right now, we don't know shit, and we gotta treat the case that way. As far as I'm concerned, everyone's a suspect."

Clyde nodded. "Right. We need to keep an open mind."

"Can you do that?" Sam asked. "Or is that gonna be a problem?"

Clyde shook his head and fixed Sam with a stern look. "You don't know me, so I'm gonna forgive that comment. But I assure you, I'm a professional. I am an objective officer of the law, and I take that very seriously. My personal opinions don't matter. Tomorrow, we start a full investigation. I'll have a plan ready."

Sam could tell that Clyde was in over his head but had enough pride to not want to ask Sam for help – or admit he didn't even know where to start.

"If it were up to me," Sam said, being careful not to bruise Clyde's ego. "I'd start by retracing everything we know."

Clyde nodded. "Exactly what I was thinking. We need to trade notes and theories. I'm thinking we work together."

"Or we can split up," Sam suggested. "Save time that way. But whatever you think."

Clyde frowned but then nodded in agreement. "No. No. You may be on to something. Let's do that. We'll meet in the morning, share info and split responsibilities, then divide and conquer."

"Sounds smart to me," Sam responded. "Tonight, I'll write down the people I think we need to talk to and bring it with me."

"Right," Clyde said, nodding firmly. "And I'll do the same. Let's meet at the diner. 0700."

"Seven a.m. it is," Sam replied. "You're buying the coffee."

28

———

MISS POLLY HELD A SOBBING Judy in her arms, rocking back and forth and stroking her hair. Judy leaned into the matriarch, her body limp from grief.

"That's right, sugar," Polly whispered gently. "You let it all out."

"Why would she do that?" Judy blurted out between the tears. "She was happy."

Miss Polly struggled for an answer.

"That's between her and the Lord now," she finally said, her voice as soft as worn cotton. "What matters is she's in a better place. She's finally at peace."

"What do you mean 'finally'?" Judy protested. "You knew her. She wasn't struggling with anything. She'd even found a way to live with her bad marriage."

"If I've learned anything, it's that folks only show us

what they want us to see," Polly said. "I can only imagine the deep hurt she must've been carrying to take her own life like that. Trust me. I've seen it more than once – people tucking their pain away so they don't trouble anybody. But there's only so much weight one soul can carry."

"She wouldn't do that," Judy said. "We talked about everything. She told me about all her struggles. I knew that she and Gus weren't happy, but she was always finding the sunshine in everything."

"She fooled me too, hon," Polly said.

"Why didn't I see it?" Judy cried. "I could have helped her."

Polly pulled away, putting her hands on Judy's shoulders and looking her square in the eyes.

"Now listen here, you can't talk like that," Polly said firmly. "If somebody's dead-set on hiding something, they'll hide it. You can't blame yourself for her being good at hiding her darkness."

"I should have seen it! I'm her sister."

Polly pulled Judy to her and wrapped her big arms around her.

"You poor child. You can't talk that way. You're hurting bad and hunting for someone to blame, but it is not you. You understand? Amy couldn't have asked for a better sister."

Judy fell apart at the words. She began wailing,

holding on to Miss Polly like a life buoy. Polly held her, allowing Judy to let it out. After a minute or so, the pain began to loosen its grip, Judy's sobs slowly faded to whimpers, and she pulled herself away.

"Let me get you a glass of tea," Polly said, waiting for Judy to nod before heading to the kitchen.

Judy stared at the floor, lost in her thoughts. When she finally spoke, her voice had settled a bit. "It still doesn't make sense."

"What's that, Hon?" Polly asked, returning to the room with two glasses of iced tea.

Judy took a sip and set the glass down on the coffee table.

"For Amy to do that. She didn't leave a note or nothing. And her car's still missing. Something about all this just feels wrong."

"Now listen to me," Polly said, easing back beside Judy. "You've gotta quit torturing yourself. None of this makes sense, and it never will. When someone takes their own life, they leave behind more questions than answers – little rabbit holes of 'what ifs' that'll swallow you up if you let 'em. All we can do is hold on to what we do know, grieve your sweet sister, and start the slow work of healing. Life keeps on walking. Whether we keep up with it or not is up to us. I still hurt for my Randall every day. Every morning, I wake up with a heartache. But I push it aside because the world needs me. And it needs you, too."

Judy started to protest but Polly continued. "I'm not saying you'll carry on like nothing ever happened. You'll carry her memory forever. The best you can do is learn to carry her love and not her burden. For right now, we gotta put our trust in Sheriff Wheeler and R.J. They know what they're doing. Let them sort out the how-it-happened part. You just focus on honoring your sister. And, unfortunately, grieving is a part of that."

She took Judy's hands into her own. "Now, in regard to the funeral, we both know Gus Booker ain't gonna be any help. So, I'll handle the funeral arrangements as much as you need me to. And don't fret one minute about the costs."

Judy nodded and squeezed Polly's hands in appreciation. Her mind drifted to Gus, and she wondered how he was handling the news. Was he sad? Shocked? Angry? Confused as she was? Most likely he was out celebrating. Regardless, he was definitely drunk.

29

GUS STUMBLED INTO THE HOUSE, falling to the kitchen floor in the dark. He clumsily pulled himself up and swatted at the light switch several times until he finally slapped it on. How Gus managed to drive home from the bar was a miracle in and of itself, and Lord only knew what damage he left in his wake. But none of that was rattling around in his alcohol-sloshed brain right now. He staggered to a kitchen chair and fell into it, knocking a glass off the table in the process. It shattered on the floor, and all Gus could do was stare at it.

It was one of the Scooby Doo glasses Amy collected. Gus always made fun of her for it and had only pulled this one out because everything else was dirty. But now, seeing the Mystery Van scattered in blue-and-green shards across the linoleum, he felt something in his chest twist sharp as barbed wire. And he began to cry.

It was an almost silent whimper at first as he thought about the nerdy way Amy took pride in those glasses. He had teased her but had secretly loved that little quirk about her. As the memories crept in – little things he'd never admitted meant anything – he realized he wasn't ever going to experience them again. She was really gone now. She wasn't coming back. And in that moment, for the first time ever in his life, he felt truly alone.

His whimpers grew into a cry which quickly snowballed into wails of despair. Years of buried love, sour jealousy, and misguided anger surged up all at once and dragged Gus under like an undertow. He fought for breath between the sobs, and he stood, suddenly needing more reminders of Amy.

He crashed through the living room to their bedroom, dropping to his knees in front of the dresser. Still sobbing uncontrollably, he yanked a drawer all the way out, spilling its contents across the floor. T-shirts and sweaters and shorts. He sifted through it all with a bruiser's gentleness and grabbed a handful of clothes, pulling it to his face and inhaling her scent like he needed it to live.

He pulled open another drawer and rifled through cheap jewelry, odd keepsakes, old holiday cards from her sister, and a stack of photos. Recognizing them, he sat back on his heels and tried to contain his pain. He wiped his eyes on the back of his hand and thumbed through the pictures – shots of the two of them on their Galveston honeymoon, back when life felt breezy and the world hadn't yet dug its claws into them, pulling them apart.

As he looked through them, the pangs in his heart were almost unbearable, but he kept going, almost craving the pain. Finally, he dropped the photos to the floor and hung his head, spent.

But Gus's newly released emotions had no intention of sitting still. They soon began to boil into a blind anger. His face contorted and twisted in rage.

"Why did you leave me?" he yelled, his voice cracking like dry wood.

He stood up and began to throw things — anything he could grab. A hairbrush. A lamp. Books from her nightstand. He pulled a drawer out of the nightstand and slammed it against the wall over and over, splintering the cheap paneling.

"Why? Why?" he yelled over and over.

He opened the closet and began yanking her clothes off the hangers, tossing them to the floor and across the room.

"You bitch! You selfish bitch!" he cried.

In less than a minute, he had emptied the closet. He

hurled a sundress to the ground so hard he knocked himself off balance and toppled to his knees. He stayed there, on all fours, and began pounding his fist into the floor.

"You bitch! You bitch!"

The anger slowly settled, melting back into sorrow, and his cries grew quieter. The grief returned and he lay down, face to the floor among all of Amy's belongings.

"You bitch," he whispered. "You bitch."

He kept repeating the words, his voice thinning as he lost what little energy he had left. Then, as he began to drift off into a drunken, grief-soaked stupor, he mumbled something in a final faint breath.

"I love you."

With that, he passed out. Lying on Amy's clothes, unaware of a pile of notes that had fallen from her nightstand drawer. The notes were written in thick black marker on torn scraps of paper, each carrying a different, shaky message, and every one of them signed with a chicken-scratch of a signature that was easy enough to read: SKEETER.

30

THE NEXT MORNING, Sam met Constable Clyde at 7 a.m., just as they had planned. The two of them laid out everything they knew about Amy's last day, sketching a rough timeline on Clyde's legal pad.

8 a.m. – She'd stopped at the diner and picked up two coffees to go.

8:15 a.m. – Security footage showed her walking into the courthouse. Walter said she worked through lunch and never left the office other than to go to the restroom.

5 p.m. – Walter locked the office doors at 5 p.m. and began to straighten up for the day while Amy began working on her side project, going through files and writing things down in her pink journal.

6 p.m. – Walter left, locking the office door behind

him. When he left, Amy was sitting on the floor, unidentified files spread out in front of her.

9:03 p.m. – Security footage showed Amy walking out the front door of the courthouse at the same time a car seemed to be entering the parking lot.

11:10 p.m. – A set of headlights pull into the parking lot and two sets of headlights leave, presumably when Amy's car left.

"So far, I haven't come across her car on any neighboring business's security footage around eleven," Clyde said.

"We're assuming it left the parking lot at eleven, but we can't be sure. All we really know is that it was gone the next morning when the first security guard arrived at... 7 a.m.," Sam added. "Can you keep checking other cameras? Maybe widen the radius? And you should probably look for any suspicious vehicles while you're at it."

"That kinda all sounds like P.I. stuff," Clyde protested. "Why don't you do that?"

"Because I need to go talk to Walter at the courthouse," Sam replied.

"Why don't I talk to Walter?"

"Because you know him," Sam said. "He doesn't know me, so he's nervous around me. And nervous people make mistakes. Nervous people tend to talk too much, and spill more than they mean to. Besides, you'll recognize local people's cars, and I won't."

"Alright, but you're taking the next crap job," Clyde said.

"You have my word," Sam nodded, having no intention whatsoever of living up to that deal.

Sam arrived at the courthouse about twenty minutes later. It was almost nine by now, which was perfect. Sam wanted to get to the County Records Department as soon as they opened.

He greeted a fresh-faced security guard who was cleaning the front door. The guard gave Sam a nod and a smile and opened the door for him.

"Perfect timing," he said. "I just unlocked it."

Sam nodded back and walked quickly to the County Records Department, his footsteps echoing in the empty hall. Even before he reached the office, he could tell he was too early. Looking through the glass door, he could see the office was still dark, and the door didn't budge when he pushed it.

At least I'll be first in line, he thought as he leaned against the wall and sipped his coffee.

He heard Walter Puckett before he saw him – his

jumble of keys jangling as he scurried toward the office door.

"I'm sorry. I'm sorry," Walter said. "Just thrown off these last few days."

It was only after he unlocked the door that he recognized Sam.

"It's you again," he said. "The P.I. investigating Amy's..."

Walter couldn't finish his sentence. His shoulders dropped and he shook his head.

"I still can't believe it," he said. "I barely slept at all last night."

"Yeah. It's a kick in the balls, for sure," Sam clumsily offered.

"I don't want to believe it's true," Walter said, as he flipped on the lights and hustled behind the counter, turning on the computer at the front desk and then the one at his own workstation. "Do you want any coffee?"

Sam could tell Walter was a man of habit – the kind who'd keep his routine even if the courthouse was burning behind him.

"I'm good for now," Sam said, holding up his paper coffee cup.

Walter nodded and flipped on the coffee pot. "I get it ready the night before. That way, all I have to do in the morning is hit the switch."

Lots of nervous energy, thought Sam. The man rattled like a wind chime in a summer storm.

As the coffee brewed, Walter walked back to the counter and stood across from Sam.

"So, is there some way I can help?" he asked, finally slowing down enough to breathe.

"Well, the way I investigate a disappearance is a little different than how I investigate a... a suicide."

Sam decided to go along with the suicide ruling for now. It could help disarm Walter.

"I didn't think the police normally investigated suicides," Walter said.

"Well now, I'm not the police," Sam said with a smile. "I'm just trying to help her sister make sense of it all. And I thought maybe you'd have seen a side of Amy that others did not."

"What do you mean by that?" Walter asked nervously.

Sam noticed perspiration budding along Walter's hairline. He didn't know if it was because of nervousness or the frenzied morning routine that he'd just witnessed.

"You know how it is," Sam said. "Sometimes, people wear different faces at work. They put up some walls but let others down."

Walter thought for a moment then shook his head. "Honestly, I'm as shocked as anybody. She was always so chipper. A real glass-half-full kind of person. It was one of my favorite things about her."

"She never talked about problems she was having at home?"

"She never talked about her home life at all."

"Or her husband?"

"Or that. Sometimes I'd even forget she was married."

Sam drummed his fingers on the counter, letting the pause in the conversation stretch. He'd learned that silence could sometimes pry loose more information than a dozen questions could.

"What about lunch? Did she take long lunches? Or breaks? Doctor visits? Call in sick a lot? Anything unusual?"

Walter smiled. "Amy barely left the office. She'd bring her lunch almost every day, and I don't think she ever took a sick day. I had to practically force her to use vacation time."

"When was the last time she did that?" Sam asked.

"Probably about a year ago," Walter said. "I think she went with her sister to San Antonio or something."

"Not her husband?"

Walter shook his head. "If you ask me, she didn't do much of anything with him. Kind of sad. She deserved so much better."

He looked up at Sam. "You think that could be why she did what she did?"

Sam shrugged. "It's possible."

He drank the last of his coffee and sat the paper cup on the counter. "Maybe I will take a little refresher."

Walter nodded, looking back at the coffee pot to see if it had finished brewing. "Any cream or sugar?"

"Black's fine," Sam said.

Walter tossed the paper cup into the trash. "I'll get you a real coffee cup."

He poured one for Sam then another for himself, adding plenty of cream and sugar to his.

"You told me Amy stayed late working on a pet project," Sam said.

Walter nodded and brought both mugs back to the counter.

"Yes, sir. Looking at old property deeds."

"Do you mind if I take a look?"

Walter hesitated. "Technically, you probably shouldn't. Only county employees are supposed to handle the actual deeds."

"Well, if you want, I'll let you technically handle them," Sam said. "I just want to get a sense of what she was doing and I figured you probably had better things to do. If you point me toward the right cabinets, I promise not to tell anyone."

Walter mulled it over, then motioned for Sam to follow him around the counter.

An hour later, Sam was rifling through yet another file cabinet. Handicapped by a mountain of documents and no real sense of what he was looking for, everything had begun to blend together.

"So, you have no idea what section she was looking at?" he asked for probably the tenth time.

"I told you; she put everything back. If we had her journal, we'd have a better idea. She was always scribbling notes as she went."

Sam shut another file drawer and thought to himself.

"Where are the most recent files?" he asked.

Walter pointed to the file cabinet on the far right. "Over there. But Amy was always interested in the history of the area."

"Maybe she expanded her search," Sam said. Truth be told, he was grabbing at straws.

"We store all the new deeds digitally," Walter said. "But we keep the originals here."

Sam opened the top drawer and flipped through a few files, looking for anything that jumped out. It didn't take long before something did.

"Most of these properties are owned by Polly Wheeler," he said.

31

An hour later, Carla Lawson strode down the stairs of the Burdett General Hospital, where the county morgue was located. She carried herself with the same polished professionalism and quiet, immovable confidence that had helped her bulldoze through the good ol 'boys' wall of law enforcement for years. She knew R.J. Sanders wasn't happy about having her assist on a second autopsy — an autopsy that he didn't feel was warranted. But Carla had convinced him that the involvement of a renowned medical examiner might silence the second-guessers and keep an already messy case from sprouting new problems.

She knew he'd only agreed because refusing her would've looked worse, so she walked down the hallway to the morgue fully aware she wasn't exactly a welcome sight.

Story of most of my professional life, she thought, unbothered.

R.J. was already prepping the body when Carla opened the door. He was an elderly African American man, with closely cropped gray hair and matching beard. Carla figured him to be in his eighties – putting him well past retirement age. That meant he either really loved his job, or he was a stubborn man who didn't like being told what to do. Either way, she would have to play her cards carefully to get his cooperation.

"You're late," the old man muttered.

Carla checked her watch. "I'm right on time."

"If you're on time, you're late."

"So, you're a Vince Lombardi fan?" she asked with a grin, hoping her knowledge of the source of the quote might soften his edges — especially since it was a football reference.

When in doubt, always go with football, she thought.

He smirked at her reply.

Mission accomplished.

She grabbed a lab coat from a hook and moved to the other side of the body.

"You wanna drive?" he muttered. "Or are you gonna be a backseat driver?"

"I'm here to assist," she said diplomatically. "This is

your autopsy. I just figure I might be useful, seeing as I've probably handled more homicide cases than you.

"Don't go making assumptions," R.J. said. "I was poking at dead bodies before you were born. And who said anything about murder? This young lady hung herself. Body found swinging from a rope. No other wounds on her body."

"Sounds like a theory," Carla replied. "Let's prove it. Are you recording this?"

"I write it down as I go," R.J. replied.

"Mind if I record?" Carla asked. "It's just easier, especially once our hands get messy."

"Don't see why your hands are gonna get messy, but help yourself," R.J. shrugged.

Carla grabbed her recorder and clicked it on, stated Amy's full name along with the time and date, then set it on a table near the exam slab.

Even though she'd said she'd assist, she couldn't help herself. She leaned in first, examining the neck wound. A hanging victim with a beating heart would've shown bruising beneath the ligature mark. But Amy's skin showed only a red indentation.

"There's an absence of vital reaction in the ligature mark," Carla said loudly.

"Why are you yelling?" R.J. scowled. "I may be old, but I ain't deaf."

"For the recorder," Carla said.

R.J. shook his head and returned to the body.

"No sign of hemorrhage in the neck musculature," Carla added. "And her pallor is more uniform than what you'd expect from a hanging."

R.J. was clearly annoyed by Carla dominating the examination, but Carla didn't seem to notice.

"You had noted lividity in your initial report but didn't note where it occurred," she said, checking and poking the body. "But I'm seeing lividity is fixed in the back and buttocks and back of the thighs. If she'd died by hanging, it would be found in the hands, forearms and lower extremities."

"So, you're saying she didn't hang herself," he asked. "Ma'am, I was there. I helped pull her body down."

"She was hanging for sure," Carla said. "But both of those indicators point to postmortem suspension."

"So, she died then she hung herself," R.J. scoffed. "You know how stupid that sounds? She weren't shot. She weren't stabbed. Not a bruise on her."

"Well, that's why we need to take a closer look," Carla replied. "This is the fun part. This is where we get to play detective."

"There ain't nothing fun about examining the body of someone you know," R.J. snapped. "And I'd appreciate it if you'd show this young lady some respect instead of treating her body like a game of Clue."

Carla walked around the body, looking under fingernails, in the mouth and in the ears.

"You always take the sheriff at his word?" she said. "Why even conduct an autopsy then?"

R.J. shook his head. "I used to be like you," he said. "All cocky and full of fight. Maybe you need to be in a big city. You're from New Orleans, right? Probably had a full team, too. Didn't you? This is a small, sleepy county in East Texas, ma'am. I know the sheriff and I trust him. And I pulled her body down myself. Sometimes, it's as simple as it looks."

"Well, this looks anything but simple," Carla replied, pointing to one of Amy's ears. "Look in the ear canal. There's dirt. But the body is clean."

R.J. took the otoscope from Carla and leaned down to look in the ear.

"Also, there seems to be some fragments in the back of her hair. Blue polyethylene maybe? My guess is a tarp or something."

R.J. followed along, embarrassed by all the evidence he had overlooked.

"So, if she didn't hang herself, how are you proposing she died?" R.J. asked.

"I don't know yet," Carla replied calmly. "But the answers may be inside. Would you like the honors?"

After prepping the body for an internal examination, R.J. begrudgingly cut an incision down the sternum and opened the chest cavity. Carla leaned in immediately.

"What are we looking for?" R.J. asked, maneuvering to get a look.

Carla moved her hands through the organs. "The body had five days to decompose before it was found, correct?"

"That's right. Unless you want to second guess that, too," R.J. muttered.

"No, I agree with your determination," Carla said. "That just means this part's a little trickier. But there are still signs to look for."

She lifted a lung slightly.

"Lungs appear heavy," Carla said for the recorder. "Can you hold this?"

R.J. held one of the lungs as Carla sliced into it.

"I'll be damned," he murmured.

"Frothy bronchial secretions present in the lungs," Carla said.

"What the hell would cause that?" R.J. asked.

"I have some thoughts," Carla replied. She picked up a scalpel and began slicing carefully down the body's throat.

"My Lord, woman," R.J. said.

"I need to examine her trachea," Carla explained. "Yep. Noting copious bloody secretions in the trachea."

"You think she was poisoned?" R.J. asked.

"Sure is starting to look like it," Carla said. "Unfortunately, decomposition may have contaminated the blood."

"So, it's just a theory," R.J. said.

"For now," Carla said. "We might get more reliable results from the liver."

"What are we looking for there?" R.J. asked.

"We're not," Carla replied. "But we can send a sample to get it tested. You want me to fill out the order?"

"I'm more than capable of filling out a toxicology request," R.J. grumbled.

Carla nodded, both of them knowing full well she was going to double-check it.

32

———

SAM'S PHONE rang as he slid into the cab of his truck. He answered the call and put it on speaker, sliding the phone under the large rubber band he'd put around his center console to hold it steady.

"Hey, baby," he answered. "How's the autopsy going?"

"We're done," Carla replied.

"Already?" Sam asked, shocked. "You decide to phone it in, too?"

"Didn't take very long to find everything we could. The rest has been sent out for tests."

"So, what did you find out?" Sam asked.

"The big news is she didn't hang herself," Carla replied. "She was already dead before the rope ever touched her neck."

Her announcement hit just as he had turned the ignition, sending classic rock blaring through the speakers. Sam fumbled to turn the radio off, but only succeeded in flipping to a country station, then to talk radio where two men were yelling at each other. He finally killed the engine to quiet everything.

They both took a second to recover from the assault by radio.

"Could you say that again?" he asked nonchalantly. "I think I missed some of it."

"No bruising around the rope mark. No signs of petechiae or facial congestion. Lividity in her back instead of lower extremities," Carla said. "All very obvious indicators that she was dead before a rope was ever put around her neck."

"So, how did she die?" Sam asked.

"Based on evidence found in the lungs and esophagus, my guess is poison," Carla said. "But I can't be sure. R.J. sent out samples for a full tox report, but that could take a few days. And the decomposition already contaminated a lot of the blood."

"So, we may not find out," Sam said.

"It gets worse," Carla admitted. "There are literally hundreds of toxins, and toxicology can't test for all of them."

"It only tests the most common ones," Sam nodded.

"Right. Without knowing what we're looking for, it's almost impossible to guess the right ones."

"Almost impossible," Sam interjected.

"Well, I have a few guesses," Carla replied. "But there's simply no way to know until we know."

"But we do know she didn't hang herself," Sam said. "That's enough to get the sheriff to start treating this like a homicide. You're the best."

"Don't you forget it," Carla replied.

"So... what are you gonna do now? Heading back home?"

"Sam Lawson! I am literally in the same town as you and you don't want to see me?"

"Well, I didn't want to assume."

"You're my husband," Carla laughed. "You get to assume once in a while."

"In that case, want to a-zooom back to my motel room?"

"I'm already parked outside of your door," Carla said with a grin in her voice. "How fast can you get here?"

"Five minutes tops," Sam stammered, firing up the engine and barreling out of the parking lot.

An hour later, the couple lay on top of the tousled sheets staring up at the dingy ceiling, marked with old, rusty water stains.

"You got yourself a real dump here, honey," Carla deadpanned.

"The Ritz was booked," Sam quipped. "Besides, the bed bugs keep me company at night."

"I pray to God you're kidding," she said, kissing him before slipping out of bed.

Sam took advantage of the moment to appreciate Carla's toned, naked body.

"I think you keep getting sexier and sexier," he said.

"That's because you've only been sharing your bed with bugs the last couple of nights," Carla replied, picking her bra and panties off the floor and shaking them out before putting them back on.

"I'm serious," Sam said. "Even after you ruined everything by putting on clothes, you're still the sexiest woman I've ever seen."

Carla picked Sam's underwear off the floor and tossed it at his chest.

"I don't know if I would call these clothes but thank you."

She gathered the rest of her outfit and went into the bathroom.

"This is when you tell me that I'm the sexiest man you've ever seen," Sam called after her.

"What's that?" Carla teased from behind the bathroom door. "I can't hear you, babe. Must be those bed bugs."

Sam chuckled, sitting up to get dressed.

"So, what's on your agenda the rest of the day?" Carla asked.

"Next stop is the sheriff's office," Sam said. "You wouldn't want to come with me, would you? No telling what R.J. told him about the autopsy."

Carla stepped back out wearing dark blue slacks and a crisp white blouse. She looked like she belonged in a courtroom. Sam, in his jeans and untucked denim shirt, looked like he'd wandered out of a feed store. She gave him a once-over and shook her head.

"I can see how I might be able to lend some credibility," she said. "You ever hear the expression 'Dress to impress. Dress for success.'?"

Sam grinned. "You ever hear 'Dress for the person you want to be.'?"

Carla stepped close and slid her arms around his neck, kissing him deeply.

"And who do you want to be, Sam Lawson," she purred.

"It's not so much who I want to be, but where I want to be," he said, kissing her neck and then down the front of her blouse until he was kneeling in front of her.

Carla let out a breathy gasp as he slid her slacks' zipper down.

33

The late-morning sun peaked uneasily through the grimy blinds in Gus Booker's bedroom, catching dust motes drifting above the disaster he'd made of the place the night before. Clothes were scattered everywhere, with a mound heaped across the bed. The shattered remnants of the nightstand drawer lay against the far wall.

Gus still lay on the floor, half-curled up on top of one of Amy's sweaters, his face mashed into the carpet. He began to stir, unsure of where he was or what time it was. The headache behind his eyes throbbed hard enough to rattle his teeth. As he slowly pulled himself up, he became aware of a loud knocking at his front door.

"Gus Booker, open this damn door!"

There was no mistaking her voice. It was Mandy.

Gus groaned and shifted, his stomach protesting any attempt at movement. Before he could get an elbow under him, he heard the door swing open, and footsteps slowly walk toward him.

"What in the hell happened in here?" Mandy muttered, her voice getting closer.

Gus pulled himself up on his knees, still leaning against the bed, just as Mandy entered the room. She froze in the doorway, hands on her hips.

"Good Lord Almighty!"

Gus's eyes tried to focus on her. She was wearing tight jeans and a buttoned-down shirt that was probably only half unbuttoned. As always, she radiated the same brash Mandy-ness that swung somewhere between confidence and wildfire.

"What are you doing here?" Gus muttered in a cracked, gravelly voice.

"Checking to make sure you made it home alive," she scoffed.

He winced and pushed himself up to sit on the bed. "I'm alive."

"Barely," Mandy said. "You look like a hungover possum that lost a fight to a lawnmower."

He rubbed his hands over his face. "Feel worse."

For a moment, she softened. She nudged aside a pair of Amy's shoes with her boot. "You really made a mess of the place," she said, quieter now. "I'm guessing you had a rough night of it?"

"I don't remember," was all he offered.

"You shouldn't be in here like this. Not by yourself."

"I don't want any company," he mumbled.

"Well, too bad," she said, walking around the bed and kneeling in front of him, her hands on his legs. "I'm not going anywhere."

Gus closed his eyes, leaning forward with his elbows on his knees. He couldn't look at Mandy without feeling a fresh stab of guilt. Mandy being here – now – felt wrong. But he didn't have the strength, or the will, to make her leave.

"You know," she began, tone smoothing to something gentle and almost caring, "you spent years telling me how miserable your marriage made you. How Amy didn't understand you. How you two were living separate lives."

Gus swallowed. Part of him bristled at her words. Part of him recognized the truth.

"That was before," he muttered.

"Before what? Before she died?" Mandy asked, trying hard to keep her voice subdued. "I don't mean to speak ill of the dead. I feel horrible about what she did.

But this guilt thing you're doing? That ain't fair to you. She wasn't sitting around crying over you. This ain't your fault."

He jerked his head up, eyes sharp. "Do not start."

"I swear to God, I'm not trying to start anything," she said, hands lifted in surrender. "I'm trying to help. I know you cared about her, even when you hated her. I know you're hurting. I ain't some cold-hearted…"

She let the words trail off, not wanting to call herself what she feared Gus was thinking. But he wasn't thinking about her at all.

"I said some awful things to her sometimes," he said.

"People say crap when they're unhappy," Mandy replied. "Doesn't mean you wanted this."

He didn't answer. He didn't know how.

"I know you, Gus Booker," she continued, softer now. "I know you better than anyone. Even her. You feel things deeper than you admit. That's one of the reasons I…" she paused, collecting herself, "one of the reasons I care about you."

He finally looked up at her. Mandy's eyes were rimmed pink, more from trying not to cry than anything. She noticed him noticing and straightened her shoulders proudly. "Point is, you can't sit in all this squalor drowning in your misery. Amy wouldn't want that. And I won't have it."

He almost laughed at that. "You didn't even like Amy."

"No," Mandy admitted. "But that don't mean I don't feel sorry for what she did. And it don't mean you deserve to drown in it."

The room went silent. There was nothing but Gus's ragged breathing and the loud hum of the refrigerator. Mandy looked around the wreckage of the bedroom. "Let me help you clean this up. I can get some bags for her things."

Gus shook his head. "No." His gaze settled on the empty closet. "Her stuff stays."

Mandy blinked, surprised by the sudden force in his voice. "Gus, it might be easier on you if we..."

"It stays," he said again, his jaw tightening. "I ain't getting rid of her things. Not yet."

"I'm not saying toss it," Mandy countered gently. "I'm saying maybe... maybe it shouldn't be the first thing you see when you walk in here. That's only gonna torture you."

"Maybe that's what I deserve," he snapped back.

"Look at me," Mandy said firmly. Her very limited patience had grown thin. "I said, look at me."

She lifted Gus's face to hers. "You do not deserve to torture yourself. Amy made the choice to kill herself. You didn't make her. And you don't know it had anything to do with you. So, stop being so caught up in your little pity party and man up."

She stood and grabbed the surviving dresser drawer that Gus had pulled out in anger. "We'll leave her stuff. For now. But we're still cleaning it up."

Gus pushed himself up, swaying slightly. "Yeah. Fine. Whatever."

Mandy slammed Amy's clothes back in the drawer, making it very clear she was not happy to be doing it. Gus was smart enough to know better than to say anything. And the two silently began cleaning up. Gus put a hand on the bed to steady himself as he bent down to gather some of the clothes he'd thrown. Picking up the sweater he had slept on, a small piece of paper fluttered. Sam looked down to see more scraps of paper, each with a note scrawled on it. He picked up a handful and read them.

THANK YOU FOR ALL YOU DO.

PLEASE STAY WITH ME.

I NEED YOU HERE.

DON'T LEAVE.

And at the bottom of each:

- SKEETER

Gus stared at them, puzzled. He knew who Skeeter was. Everyone did. But why was he writing notes to Amy? And what did he mean by "Don't Leave"? Had she confided in him?

Gus looked up to see if Mandy had noticed him reading the scraps of paper, but she was facing away from him, picking clothes off the floor on the other side of the bed. He silently slid the notes into his back pocket.

34

SAM PULLED his truck to a stop in the parking lot at the sheriff's station. He leaned back and let out a deep exhale.

"I still haven't caught my breath," he said.

"You have no one to blame except yourself," Carla teased.

"Oh, yeah. You're completely innocent," Sam countered. "If you weren't so damn hot, none of this would've happened."

"Well, I suppose I could let myself go — for your sake."

Sam shook his head. "No. No. I couldn't possibly ask you to make that kind of a sacrifice," he smirked. "It's a burden I'll have to bear."

Carla leaned over, kissed him on the cheek, then opened her door.

"Poor, pitiful you. You ready?"

Sam shot her a big grin. "You know how much I love this."

The couple walked into the station and instantly shifted into professional mode. Gone were the flirty touches and easy affection; now they moved like law enforcement colleagues. Acquaintances at best. If you didn't know better, you'd never guess they shared a bed, a mortgage, and a complicated history.

That had been Carla's rule back when they first started dating – when Sam was still a detective with the Quinton Police Force. Sam had struggled with it at first – not because he didn't understand the logic, but because being anything other than himself was not something he'd ever had any interest in doing. Eventually, though, he turned it into a private game, crafting elaborate backstories for their "work versions" of themselves. Sam was married to a librarian he'd met at a Houston PD outreach event; they had no kids but owned three Rottweilers named Henry, George and Duncan. Carla's character was a widowed medical examiner who still wore her ring and nursed a quiet crush on Sam.

Carla, understandably, didn't particularly care for Sam's imaginary soap opera.

He had agreed never to mention his made-up characters to anyone, and now that most people knew they were married, the backstories didn't even make any sense. But Sam still played them in his head for his own amusement.

Sheriff Wheeler saw the duo walk in the building and toward his office and stood to meet them at his door.

"Hello, Lawson," he said with a grin. "I see you brought your missus along."

Without missing a beat, Carla extended her hand. "Good to meet you, Sheriff. I'm Dr. Carla Lawson, Hubbard County Medical Examiner."

The sheriff shook her hand. "Now what is a beautiful woman like you doing in a dirty job like that?"

Sam saw the hair stand up on the back of Carla's neck, contradicting the warm smile that spread across her face.

"Why, thank you, Sheriff," she said, pouring on the charm. "It gets me out of the house."

"And those dead bodies probably don't talk back like your other half here does," he said, jerking a thumb at Sam.

"Oh, I don't know about that," Carla replied. "You'd be surprised at what all they have to say."

The sheriff chuckled and motioned them inside.

"Well, that's the problem, ain't it?" he said, sliding

into his chair. Sam and Carla took the two seats across from him. "What they have to say is open to interpretation."

"Not really," Carla replied. "Science doesn't interpret. It measures. It's all based on facts."

"I'm more of a 'go with your gut' kind of guy," the sheriff said. "How about you, Sam?"

"I go where my gut tells me," Sam replied. "But I let the facts point the way."

The sheriff opened a folder that had been sitting on his desk. Inside it was the coroner's autopsy report.

"I suppose you're here about this," the sheriff said. "R.J. already brought a copy over. He was pretty pissed that he was being second-guessed by a third party."

"Or was he pissed that he'd been sloppy?" Carla asked, not flinching.

The sheriff grinned. "I'm sure that played a part."

"Sheriff, regardless of whose toes got stepped on," Sam said. "The truth changes things. She didn't hang herself. This needs to be treated like a homicide."

"It definitely *looks* like she didn't hang herself," the sheriff countered. "But that don't mean it was murder."

"What? You think she died then turned into some kind of zombie, and hung herself before she started eating brains?" Sam asked. "Someone staged it. They hung her body, and odds are pretty good that whoever did it was her killer."

"I agree it's suspicious," the sheriff said. "And I'm treating it as such. But we need to wait for toxicology before we start jumping to conclusions. Follow the facts. Right, Mrs. Lawson?"

"The facts may help determine the exact cause of death," Carla replied. "But they also prove she was dead before someone staged a hanging. And that bears a full investigation."

"You're misunderstanding me," the sheriff said, his voice dripping with condescension. "I agree with you. I'm opening a full investigation. Chances are very likely she was murdered. But I'm going to keep an open mind to all possibilities."

"And do nothing," Sam snapped. "You need to call the Rangers or bring someone in who can actually help you investigate."

"I know how to do my job, Mr. Lawson," the sheriff said sharply. "I want to find out what happened to Amy Booker as much as you do. Maybe more. Keep in mind this is my town. She grew up here. Her and her sister both. We all went to the same church. You didn't."

He turned to Carla. "R.J. tells me you think she was poisoned."

"Her autopsy suggested signs consistent with that," Carla answered, trying her hardest to remain professional, even though she knew she was being railroaded.

"So, if you're right, this toxicology test would prove it," the sheriff replied.

"Toxicology only screens for common toxins," Carla replied. "If the killer used something other than one of those common poisons, it won't show up. But negative results do not equal no poison. If we know the poison, we can test for that particular toxin."

"I know how it works," the sheriff said. "Gotta know what she was poisoned with before you can test to see if she was poisoned. Not the most efficient system."

"At present, it's all we have," Carla said.

"So, you're saying we don't know how she died, and we may never know."

"You know enough to know that someone else was involved," Sam interjected. "Someone had to hang her body in that basement. We need to be looking for that person."

"First off, there is no *we* here, son," the sheriff snapped. "You're not law enforcement. You're a hired investigator. The very fact that I'm sitting here talking to you is a courtesy."

"Sheriff Wheeler, I think what Mr. Lawson is saying makes sense," Carla offered.

"I didn't say it didn't," the sheriff replied. "But I won't sit here and be told how to do my job by an ex-cop and a fake doctor."

Before Carla could snap back, Sam attempted to lower the temperature in the room.

"You're right," he said. "I'm sorry. I crossed a line. Old habits, right?"

Sam tried to ignore the frosty glare Carla was throwing at him. But his honey-over-vinegar approach seemed to work. The sheriff's clenched jaw relaxed and he nodded in agreement.

"We'll get out of your hair," Sam said, standing. "I know your hands are full."

He paused at the door.

"Oh, one more question. Totally unrelated. Pure curiosity."

"Shoot," the sheriff said.

"Well, I was at County Records, where Amy worked," Sam said. "She'd been digging through old land deeds. Some weird hobby that makes no sense to me. Anyway, I couldn't help but notice Polly Wheeler's name on a lot of them. She's been buying up quite a bit of real estate."

The sheriff stared, waiting for more.

"Just struck me as odd," Sam continued. "I was wondering what you knew about that."

The sheriff studied Sam. Finally, his familiar grin spread across his face.

"Last I checked, there weren't no law against investing in real estate," the sheriff said. "Miss Polly got into it after her husband died. I guess you could call it her hobby."

"Not as weird as Amy's, for sure. But that's gotta cost her a lot of money," Sam said. "You know where she gets all her money?"

"Well, that's a private matter and, frankly, none of our business," the sheriff said. "Maybe it was from the life insurance from when Randall died."

"Randall?"

"Her late husband, God rest his soul."

"Did he have family money" Sam asked.

The sheriff burst out laughing. "Good Lord, no. If he did, my daddy's got some explaining to do."

Amused at the couple's confused faces, he leaned forward and lowered his voice like he was sharing a secret.

"Randall was my brother. Miss Polly is my sister-in-law."

35

"WELL, THAT WAS FRUSTRATING," Carla said, sliding back into Sam's truck. "Do you really think he's going to investigate this as a murder?"

Sam shut her door then walked around to the driver's side, climbing in behind the wheel.

"Maybe. Maybe not. But I sure as hell don't trust him," Sam replied, pulling out his phone and tapping in a number. "Luckily for us, the sheriff is not the only badge in this county. We've still got the constable."

Clyde answered his phone on the first ring.

"Sam, I was about to call you."

Clyde was standing in a small dirt parking lot by the entrance to a state park, a handful of people milling around behind him.

"Where have you been?" Sam asked, putting the

phone on speaker so Carla could hear. "Please tell me you've got good news."

"I'm out at Sandy Ridge State Park," Clyde replied. "You should get out here."

"Why? Did you find anything?"

"I don't trust the phone lines," Clyde said. "I'll text you the address."

Carla raised an eyebrow. "He doesn't trust the phone lines?"

Sam shrugged. "To know Constable Clyde is to love him."

Thirty minutes later, Sam pulled into the lot. A cluster of trucks and cars filled the space, and the constable's SUV was parked crookedly near the trees. Before Sam could kill the engine, Clyde was already hustling toward them.

"Clyde, this is Carla Lawson," Sam said as they stepped out of the truck. "She's a medical examiner."

"And your wife," Clyde added, shaking her hand enthusiastically. "You're the one keeping this case alive. Thank you so much. I only got the big picture, but I'd love to pick your brain about everything you found."

Sam cut him off. "Why did you drag us out here, Clyde?"

"So," Clyde began proudly, "I expanded my perimeter of security cameras like we talked about, and this particular little parking lot dawned on me."

He pointed to a lopsided security camera staring uselessly at the road.

"You couldn't tell me that on the phone?" Sam asked.

"I wanted you to see how empty it is," Clyde said, exasperated. "And notice where the camera is pointing. Storms must have knocked it around and nobody bothered fixing it. So, now it's pointing out toward the road."

"Okay," Sam said. "I've got the visual. You wanna fill in the gaps?"

Clyde pulled out his phone and opened his map app, holding it out so Sam and Carla could look over his shoulder at it.

"I realized this lot sits real close to Skeeter's home," he said, pointing past a thick clump of pine trees. "It's literally half a mile straight through those woods."

He looked at Sam to see if he was following along. Sam's blank stare told him he was not.

"I checked the security footage from that camera. There's hardly been any traffic on this road the past five days. Most of it coming this way, from the direction of Skeeter's house, not toward it. If somebody drove to the house, they would've been on the footage. And the only car of note was the Ford Bronco that belonged to those teens. If, however, a car turned into this parking lot…"

"The camera wouldn't have caught them," Sam finished.

"Someone could've brought Amy's body here and carried her through the woods to the house," Carla said.

Clyde practically bounced. "Yes!"

"I've got volunteers combing the woods, looking for any evidence that could have been left behind."

Sam studied the dirt in the lot, imprinted with dozens of tire tracks going in different directions.

"So, there's no way we can look for tire tracks at this point," Sam said.

"I'm not an idiot. I checked for that first," Clyde said. "There weren't any."

"Then no one parked here," Sam replied.

"I said there weren't any tire tracks," Clyde said. "There was nothing. There would have been something. The lot had clearly been brushed clean."

Sam grinned, unable to resist. "So I guess someone literally covered their tracks."

Clyde shook his head, frustrated that Sam wasn't taking him seriously.

"Man, tough crowd," Sam said, shifting gears as he looked at the wall of trees. "How thick are those woods?"

"Pretty thick. Wouldn't be an easy hike, especially carrying a dead body."

"So, they'd have to be in good shape," Sam said, thinking out loud.

"Amy was petite," Clyde said. "She wouldn't have weighed a lot."

"Someone could have dragged her," Carla suggested.

"We haven't found any evidence of that," Clyde said. "My volunteers have been looking for hours for anything – broken branches, piece of fabric, anything. So far, nothing."

"There could have been two people," Sam said. "Either way, our killer must have known about the security camera, or they'd have just driven up to the house."

"And they'd have to know these woods would lead to the house," Clyde said.

"Hang on," Carla said. "Your new evidence is new security footage that doesn't show anything so it makes this parking lot suspicious except there were no tire tracks and no sign whatsoever of someone carrying a body through the woods."

"Well, when you say it like that," Sam muttered.

"It's a long shot, I admit," Clyde said.

"I need to take a look at the house," Sam said.

"Sheriff's already sealed it off," Clyde said.

"And he's made it very clear that I am not a part of the investigation," Sam said, a hint of resignation in his voice.

Clyde straightened, lifting his chin. "I, on the other hand, am an elected law enforcement official of Burdett County. He can't stop me from taking a look."

36

———

WHILE CLYDE ATTEMPTED to get into Skeeter's house to look for evidence, Sam needed to follow up on something else – and Carla could prove invaluable.

They pulled up to Walter's modest house just after six. The county clerk answered the door and hurried them inside.

"Hurry," he said. "I don't want anyone to see you."

"Walter, I take great offense to that," Sam said. "You don't know me well enough yet to be embarrassed of me."

"I'm just nervous," he said. The sweaty brow and jittery mannerisms instantly confirmed it. "I could get into a lot of trouble for this."

"Who's this?" he asked, nodding toward Carla.

"This is my wife, Carla," Sam said. "She might be able to help us. Were you able to get everything?"

"A lot of it," Walter said, motioning them to the dining room where the table was covered in files. "This is all the property deeds in Burdett County for the past ten years. Any more would have raised too much suspicion."

"This is hopefully plenty," Sam said, surveying the mass of paper.

"Sam filled me in on everything," Carla said. "I'm pretty good at catching details and patterns. If there's something hidden in all this, we should be able to find it. Can you walk me through how to read a deed?"

"Mind if I hit the can?" Sam asked.

Walter pointed him down the hallway, turning back to explain the different components of a deed to Carla. Sam headed toward the bathroom slowly, taking in the house with a detective's eye.

The old floors creaked under his boots. The walls were covered in dank, faded wallpaper. The furniture was just as old. A large wooden China cabinet displayed a mismatched array of delicate plates and porcelain figurines. Looking into the living room, Sam could see the gold fabric couch, sagging slightly in the middle. He smiled at the familiar sight of a crocheted Afghan draped over the back of it. It had the gold and brown zig-zag pattern that made it a staple of just about every grandmother's home in the 1970s. In fact, if Sam didn't know any better, he'd have guessed someone's grandmother still lived here. But Walter had already told him that he had inherited the house from his grandmother. Apparently, he inherited her commitment to never changing anything.

The hallway walls were covered with old photographs of people who were most-likely family members. From their dated hairstyles and clothes, it was obvious none of the photos were recent. There was one picture in an oval frame of an awkward looking boy in a sweater vest and tragic bowl cut. Sam recognized the sad eyes instantly as Walter's.

He walked past the bathroom to the room at the end of the hallway, which had to be the bedroom. Sam stepped in quietly, hoping to get a peak while Walter was preoccupied with Carla. Luckily, there was still enough sunlight that he didn't need to hit the wall switch. Sam stood in the doorway and looked around. It was as dated as the rest of the house and Sam half-wondered if Norman Bates lived here. But other than the creepiness of it all, nothing unusual jumped out at him... until he turned toward the dresser.

And froze.

Carla and Walter sifted through the deeds, looking for patterns or anything unusual. They hadn't been at it long when Carla stopped.

"I'm looking at the deeds for the properties Polly Wheeler owns, and I can't find any bill of sales."

Walter looked at a file she handed him.

"Oh. That's because she inherited them," Walter said.

He flipped through a file to a different document and showed it to her. Carla went back through the other files and found similar paperwork.

"She inherited a lot of property," Carla said.

Walter nodded. "The way I understand it, people left their property in their will as a way to pay her back."

"Pay her back for what?" Carla asked.

Walter shrugged. "Miss Polly helps folks out all the time. She'd find odd jobs to help them make extra money. Find them a place to live. Give out loans to help them get back on their feet. But most people are living paycheck to paycheck and don't have much to spare. So, instead of loan payments, they'd put her in their will and leave her their land when they died."

"How many properties has she inherited?"

"I couldn't say," Walter replied. "It's pretty common around here. Folks leaving their property to pay off a debt."

"What if they have living relatives? Do they lose their home?"

Walter chuckled. "Oh, Miss Polly would never do that. She doesn't kick anybody out. In fact, she'll fix up the place for them."

"What if they still have a mortgage?"

"Polly would buy it out. Never was much money and, I'm guessing she worked up a good deal with the bank. The manager is her first cousin."

"Walter," Sam said, reappearing so suddenly both Carla and Walter jumped. "Why the hell are their pictures of Amy taped to your bedroom mirror?"

Walter looked like a kid that had just got caught cheating on a test. His face turned bright red and his gaze ping-ponged from Carla to Sam.

"I, uh, it's not what it looks like," he stammered.

"No. It's exactly what it looks like," Sam said. "You've got at least a half dozen pictures of Amy, and from the way she's never looking at the camera, I'm guessing she didn't know you took them."

Walter swallowed hard, staring down at the table, unable to make eye contact with anyone.

"Were you stalking her?" Sam demanded.

"No!" Walter pleaded. "It's not like that."

Sam pulled out a chair next to Walter and sat down. "Then, please – tell us what it is like."

Walter had gone from bright red to ghost white. He began to absentmindedly rock back and forth.

"I just thought she was so great," he admitted. "I only took a few pictures."

"I counted seven," Sam interjected.

"And that's all of them," Walter insisted. "It was just... all I could have of her."

"Did you have a crush on Amy?" Carla asked gently.

"I think that's safe to say," Sam muttered sarcastically, earning a laser glare from a more compassionate Carla.

Walter nodded, still staring at the table. "I loved her," he said. "But I was never inappropriate. Ever. I respected her too much for that."

"Did she know how you felt?" Carla asked.

Walter shook his head. "I never said anything. She was married."

"But you'd sneak pictures to hang in your bedroom," Sam said. "For what? Late night inspiration?"

"Don't talk that way about Amy," Walter said, anger bubbling through the shame. "She was the only bright spot in my life. I mean, look around. And my job's as boring as it sounds. I basically sleepwalk through life. But Amy..."

His expression softened, and Sam saw the awkward kid from the hallway photo.

"When she started working at the courthouse, it was like someone opened the curtains. She was sunshine. She gave me a reason to get up in the morning."

"So, what happened?" Sam pressed. "You told her how you felt? She rejected you and you lost it? It was an accident. You didn't mean for it to happen."

Walter looked at Sam, horrified. He jumped up. "No! God, no! First off, I would never have told her how I felt. I knew she didn't see me that way and it would ruin what we did have. She'd probably leave. I needed her to just be there. And I would never - NEVER - hurt her in any way."

Sam studied Walter's face. He was nervous, unstable, and emotionally scrambled. But Sam believed him. At least for now.

Pictures on a mirror wouldn't be enough cause for a search warrant. But they were enough to keep Walter on Sam's radar. Right now, however, he needed him for the task at hand, so he was willing to give him a generous benefit of the doubt.

But knowing Walter could be leading him on a wild goose chase to throw him off the scent, Sam needed to do a bit more digging, even if that meant kicking at a hornet's nest.

37

THE NEXT MORNING, Sam met Clyde for coffee at the diner again. Carla had driven back home to grab some extra clothes. Sam had only packed for a fishing weekend and was now on Day 5 of an unplanned homicide investigation.

Clyde was already hunched over a mug at the diner when Sam walked in. The dark bags under the constable's eyes said everything.

"Up all night?" Sam asked, sliding into the booth.

He hardly felt any better. He and Carla had been at Walter's late, sifting through deeds and compiling lists.

"I didn't find anything," Clyde muttered. "I went through the house and yard, looking for any sign of anything. But the sheriff had already brought in a forensics team, and they had pretty much swept the place already."

"At least he brought in some people," Sam said.

"He didn't have a choice," Clyde said. "You kinda forced his hand with that new autopsy report."

Sam smiled. "Good. I don't care why he does his job, as long as he does it. Was he there? Did you tell him your theory?"

"I saw him," Clyde said. "But I didn't tell him anything. I don't trust him, Sam."

"You two have a bit of a rivalry, don't you?" Sam asked.

"We have different ideas of what law enforcement means," Clyde replied stiffly.

"What about the woods? Any progress there?" Sam asked.

Clyde shook his head. "Nothing. We had to stop when it got dark. I didn't want flashlights out there drawing attention until I feel my theory holds water."

"The fact that no vehicle showed up on that security footage is pretty solid," Sam argued. "Amy's body had to get to the house some way."

But Clyde shook his head. "We need more. The sheriff's a good ol' boy. He's gonna protect his friends. Or big donors. As far as I'm concerned, anyone could have done this to Amy. I don't want him involved until I'm sure he can't shield anyone."

"Can't you just go around him?" Sam asked. "Contact the Rangers or something?"

Clyde snorted. "Unfortunately, I've already tried that way too many times," he said. "I'm their boy who cried wolf now. They hang up as soon as they hear my name."

"Maybe I can make some calls," Sam said. "But right now, I need your help with something else."

He slid a notepad across the table.

"What's this?" Clyde asked.

"Those are all the people who died and left their property to Polly Wheeler," Sam said. "You recognize any of them?"

Clyde nodded. "I recognize all of 'em. This is a small county, Sam."

"What is she doing with all that land?" Sam asked.

Clyde gave a half-smile. "I assure you, it's not as sinister as it looks. Some people around here have long used their property as collateral for loans because that's all they had. Banks wouldn't help them. But Polly would. If they died still owing, she kept the property."

"Yeah, I can read the deeds."

"But it was more than that," Clyde said. "Most of those people died with spouses or kids that are still alive. Banks would've kicked them out. But when it becomes Polly's property, she handles it differently. She works out deals with the survivors. Lets them pay what they can so they can keep living there."

"I don't get it. What does she get out of it?" Sam asked.

"I don't know. A cushier seat in heaven?" Clyde replied with a shrug. "I'm assuming once the survivor dies or moves, she gets the land. But I can't imagine she's in it for the money. There are all kinds of better ways to do that."

"So, she's just helping people out?" Sam asked.

"People do that, Sam," Clyde said with a smirk. "As hard as it is to believe."

Sam stared at the list, unconvinced. He was having a hard time believing someone could be *that* charitable.

"New question," he said. "How many of these names had survivors? And how many of them are still alive?"

Clyde looked through the list. "I know spouses. But there could be grown kids I don't know about."

"Let's start with spouses then. How many had surviving husbands or wives? And how many of them are still alive?"

Clyde went through the first two pages of the list. He pointed out that about three quarters of those names had a surviving wife or husband. And about half of those were now dead.

"Doesn't that seem strange to you?" Sam asked.

"Most of them are old people, Sam," Clyde

answered. "That's what they do. I still don't see where you're going with this. What about finding Amy's killer?"

"This could be connected," Sam said. "I think these are the files Amy was looking at when she got killed. Maybe she found something she shouldn't have."

Sam knew he was grasping, but it was all he had. There was a possibility that Walter might've lied about Amy's project to throw him off. But there was definitely something here. What that was, he did not have a clue.

"We've got a murder to solve," Clyde insisted.

"And this may help solve it," Sam said. "I just need you to point me to a few of the survivors. People that lost their home to Polly but are still living there."

"I need to get back to the woods," Clyde said. "I was hoping you were going to help me."

"I will," Sam said. "Just let me check this out first. A handful of names. I want to ask them a few questions."

Clyde groaned loudly, grabbed a pen from his pocket and began circling names and scribbling notes beside each one. After two sheets, he pushed the notepad over to Sam.

"There," Clyde said. "All of those people have a surviving family member that still lives on the property. I wrote down their name and relation."

Sam scanned the list. One name jumped out.

Lila Mae Garrett.

38

IT WAS a little after eight a.m. when Sam drove back to Cypress Meadows. His truck was becoming a familiar sight in the area, and residents no longer tracked him with suspicious eyes.

As he rolled slowly down the dirt road toward Lila Mae Garrett's home, another truck approached from the opposite direction. Sam eased to the side to let it pass. The driver was Toby. He slowed even more as he passed, giving Sam a long, narrow-eyed glare as he crept by.

Sam ignored it or tried to. He already knew Toby wasn't gonna be sending him any Christmas cards. But when he checked his rear-view mirror, he saw Toby's truck pull over to the shoulder and idle.

What's he waiting for? Sam wondered. *To see if I was heading toward his home?*

Sam decided to continue on his way and pulled in front of Lila Mae's home. He glanced at the rear-view mirror again as Toby's truck pulled back on the road and drove away.

Sam wasn't sure what to think. On one hand, it only fed his suspicions about Toby. On the other hand, there was no doubt Toby knew about Amy's death by now. And word was probably spreading fast that it wasn't a suicide. Maybe Toby had simply stopped out of curiosity.

But Sam didn't have time to think about all that right now. Lila Mae had already opened her door and was staring at him.

"What brings you back here, Mr. Lawson?" she asked as he stepped out of his truck. "And where's my Clyde?"

"Clyde is out saving the world," Sam said. "I'm just following up on a few things and thought you could help me. Do you have a minute?"

"Is this about Amy Booker?" Lila Mae said, lowering her head. "God rest her soul. Come on in."

Sam followed her inside. The floor groaned beneath his weight, flexing slightly. It was an old house and was definitely showing signs of its age – sun-faded plywood walls, green carpet worn thin as paper, and peeling laminate on the kitchen floor. But Lila Mae did her best to keep it all presentable. The thrift-store furniture was clean, and the walls were adorned with family photos. The lemony scent of a fresh cleaning hung in the air.

Lila Mae coughed as she motioned to the couch for Sam to sit. She settled into a wooden rocking chair across from him. The couch protested loudly as Sam sat, and he worried he might end up on the floor.

"I apologize for this dang cough," she said. "I think it's the allergies or something. But don't worry. I ain't contagious. Now what can I help you with?"

"You have a wonderful home, Mrs. Garrett," Sam said. "How long have you lived here?"

"Please call me Lila Mae," she said warmly. "And I guess I've lived here for close to thirty years now. My late husband, Efrem, and I had a place in town, but a fire took it out. Then we stayed with his mama a while. But when his sister got a divorce, she and her three kids moved in. Now, I love children. I spent my life teaching them. But it was too small a house for all of that energy."

"So, you got a mortgage for this place?" Sam asked.

"Yes, sir," Lila Mae said proudly. "The Lord had decided that we weren't meant for children of our own, so we didn't need much room. This place was perfect. Back then, we didn't have near as many neighbors. We loved it. Those were good years."

She looked around her home at invisible memories, smiling as they played out in front of her. She coughed again, scattering the nostalgia and bringing her back to the present.

"Can I ask what happened to your husband?"

"He passed about five years ago," Lila Mae said softly, her eyes watering. "Got sick and never recovered. Some sort of pneumonia."

"Were you still working then?" Sam asked.

"I'd long retired. Efrem made enough at the poultry factory for both of us and he insisted. Said I'd worked hard enough and deserved to relax. My teacher's pension was just enough to cover insurance. Between that and his paycheck we were able to make it work. He was a saint, that man. Then, maybe ten years ago, he had an accident at the factory and couldn't work anymore. We tried to live on his disability as long as we could. I tried to get my job back, but there was no place for an old woman."

"But you still had bills to pay," Sam said. "Did you still have a mortgage?"

Lila Mae nodded. "I got a job at the Dollar General," she said. "It wasn't much, and barely kept the lights on, much less cover the mortgage."

"So, what'd you do?" Sam asked.

"Efrem went to see Miss Polly. Asked her for a loan, and she helped us out. I don't know what we would have done without her. Then, when Efrem died, I thought the bank was gonna take the place from me. But bless that man, he'd already worked it all out with Miss Polly. When he died, the house was put in her name. She took over the mortgage and paid for upkeep. She told me that I can live out my days here and never asked for a penny."

"She's never asked for anything in return?" Sam asked.

"Never. But I'm a proud woman and I don't want charity. I insisted on paying her what I could and insisted she write up a contract."

Lila Mae stood up and walked down the narrow hallway to the bedroom. She returned in a minute with a document and handed it to Sam.

"Got it notarized and everything," she said. "We figured out a fair amount based on my pension and Efrem's social security. I pay her $100 a month in rent with a condition that we can revisit that amount if I have some sort of medical emergency or can't afford it anymore."

"Says here the rent will never go higher and will continue until the mortgage is paid off or you pass, whichever comes first."

"Miss Polly is a godsend," Lila Mae said. "And she's done that for lots of people out here."

She coughed again. This time it was worse. Sam

went to the kitchen and grabbed a glass from a drying rack, filled it at the sink, and brought it to her. She nodded in appreciation and took a sip, letting the cough subside.

"You may wanna go check that out," Sam said.

Lila Mae waved it off. "It's from all this yapping," she said. "I tend to talk a lot. The Lord's gotta send me little reminders to take a breath every now and then."

Sam sat back down. "Can I ask you another question? What can you tell me about Skeeter?"

Lila Mae's face shifted— sadness softening her wrinkles.

"That poor soul. Life broke him, bless his heart. I've known Skeeter since we were kids, and he was always a good soul. Helping others. Always smiling. When he lost his family in that accident, something in him just clicked off. You could see it in his eyes. And you seen what's left of him now."

"Do you think he's dangerous?" Sam asked.

"Skeeter? Lord, no. He's peculiar, for sure. But there ain't no way that man is a danger, except maybe to himself."

She looked up at Sam. "Is this about Amy Booker?"

Sam was hoping she wouldn't have made the connection, but she was sharper than he thought.

"I've heard the talk," she continued. "They're saying she didn't hang herself. Did someone really kill her? Is that why you're asking about Skeeter? Let me tell you this. Anytime something bad happens, folks always rush to blame Skeeter. But I will *never* believe that about him."

Sam nodded. "I tend to agree with you," he said.

"Have you asked him yourself?" Lila Mae asked.

Sam shook his head. "We can't find him."

39

———

Sam continued to meet with people on Clyde's list the rest of the morning and into the afternoon. Everyone had a similar story. They had fallen on hard times and Miss Polly had helped them out, typically with a loan using their home as collateral. If they were unable to pay back the loan, typically because one of the spouses had died, Polly would "inherit" the home and arrange a small, very affordable rent payment for the surviving spouse.

Sam was trying not to be cynical, but either Polly Wheeler was a candidate for sainthood, or she was running the slowest, politest land grab in Texas history. Next on his agenda would be figuring out what she was doing with the property after both spouses had died.

But something else was becoming clear. Everyone

was talking about Amy's death, and nearly all of them felt like Skeeter had something to do with it. Sam knew small towns couldn't resist a bogeyman the same way cats can't resist windowsills, and Skeeter fit that part too easily. Sam had a feeling that the sheriff had already put Skeeter on his 'usual suspects' list as well. And maybe they were right. Regardless, Sam needed to find Skeeter — preferably before the sheriff did.

He had called Clyde but got no answer, so he drove out to the state park where the constable was overseeing volunteers. Hopefully they had found something that would shed new light on the case. But when Sam pulled into the parking lot, there were only three vehicles parked there, and one of them was Clyde's. It was a far cry from the packed parking lot from the day before.

He spotted the constable talking to a few men near the tree line, so he parked his truck and headed for them. Clyde saw him coming and met him halfway.

"We're just wrapping up," he said. "We couldn't find anything out of the ordinary. Nothing. Either my theory is off, or whoever did this knows these woods well enough not to leave any tracks."

"About that," Sam said, pulling Clyde aside. "Has anyone seen Skeeter the last few days?"

Clyde glanced back at the volunteers to make sure they weren't listening. "I think you and me are thinking the same thing," he said. "Skeeter's gone MIA, and nobody knows these woods - and that house - better than him."

"Do you think he's capable of doing something like this?" Sam asked.

"A week ago, I'd have said 'no way'," Clyde admitted. "But I also would've told you murders don't happen in Burdett County. I don't know what to believe anymore."

"We need to find him," Sam said. "Even if he didn't do it, he might've seen something. And we need to get to him before the sheriff uses him as his scapegoat."

"What if he did do it?" Clyde asked.

"What's his motive?" Sam asked back.

"Last I checked, crazy's a pretty good one," Clyde replied. His jaw tightened and he squared his shoulders. "I swear, if that old man did this... "

Sam could tell Clyde was working himself up.

"I'll find him," Clyde continued with a grim determination. "If he's out there, I'll bring him in."

"Don't do anything you'll regret," Sam warned. "Don't make any assumptions."

"I'll bring him in for questioning," Clyde replied. "But if he confesses to killing Amy, I'm sorry. All bets are off."

Sam didn't bother arguing. Clyde was the best chance he had, and he hoped he continued to have more bluster than bite.

Driving back into town, Sam called Carla and asked when she'd be returning.

"Probably within an hour," she said. "Are your clothes starting to stink?"

"Can't a man just miss his wife?" Sam asked with a wink.

"Oooh. That bad, huh?"

Sam was about to fire back when he saw Polly getting out of her Gold Cadillac at a gas station.

"I'll see you soon," he said, hanging up abruptly and taking a hard turn into the gas station. He pulled up to a pump opposite Miss Polly and casually slid out of his truck to gas up. Then he turned in a staged surprise toward Polly.

"Miss Polly!" he exclaimed. "I didn't expect to see you out here pumping your own gas."

Miss Polly smiled at him. "The day these stations stopped offering full service was the end of an era, for sure. Mr. Lawson, is it?"

Pretend you don't remember me, Sam observed. *A tried-and-true power move.*

"Yes, ma'am," Sam said, pouring the charm on thick. "You know I was just talking about you."

"I hear," Polly replied.

Apparently, word about his interviews had gotten

back to her quickly.

"Should I be flattered?" she asked "Is there a reason for all this curiosity?"

"I'm sorry. I'm just fascinated," Sam replied. "I had a bit of down time and wanted to wrap my head around all of your charity."

"It's a small community," Polly said. "We take care of each other."

"Looks like you're doing most of the caring," Sam said, trying to hide any of his suspicions. "These folks are lucky to have you."

Miss Polly nodded and smiled. "Well, that's very kind of you to say. But you could've just come talk to me directly."

"Funny you should say that," Sam replied. "You were on my list. I just wanted to get my facts right first."

"I'd be happy to answer any questions you may have," she replied. "But shouldn't you be working on solving Amy's death?"

Sam smiled. "Right now, there's not a lot I can do," he lied. "The sheriff has told me in no uncertain terms that this must be left to local, official law enforcement."

"I suppose there's some truth to that," Polly replied. "The sheriff is a good man. You may not fully trust him, but I can assure you Amy's case is in good hands. I tell you what, I was fixing to run to the store to make some tortilla soup for dinner. Why don't I double the recipe, and you could join me. Is your wife still in town?"

"She's heading back as we speak."

"Please bring her along," Polly said. "I'd love to meet her. The sheriff tells me she's very impressive. Sure showed up R.J. I can't say I didn't enjoy that."

Polly gave him a time and her address and told him to bring his appetite. Sam thanked her and watched as she drove off.

He didn't care so much about the land deed thing anymore. If Polly was hiding something, dinner wasn't likely to shake any truths loose. But Polly could be valuable in another way. She was the type of person who made it her business to know everything about everybody. She was sure to be a deep well of information, connections, and gossip. And that made her worth every spoonful of soup he'd have to choke down.

40

"WHAT HAVE YOU ROPED ME INTO?" Carla asked, straightening her blouse as they walked up to Polly's door.

Polly lived in an old ranch house about a mile outside of Elsip, where neighbors were separated by several acres of pasture. It was a more modest, understated home than Sam had expected. The wood siding was painted a dark maroon, accented by faded white shutters on each window. The front yard was small but lively – filled with colorful flowers and lawn decorations resembling all sorts of animals.

But even though the front yard appeared modest, Sam had noticed the property stretched far deeper behind the house. He'd noticed a large tractor shed, partially enclosed and partially open-fronted – the kind used to house farm equipment. What Sam didn't see was a farm.

Probably all left over from her husband, he noted.

Before Sam's knuckles hit the door, it flung open. Polly stood before them, grinning ear to ear.

"Well, aren't you two right on time?" she said, immediately turning her full attention to Carla. "And it is so good to meet you, darling. I hope y'all brought your appetites."

She stepped aside, letting them both in.

"Kitchen's in the back," she said. "I'm almost done."

They followed Polly through the cozy living room filled with unassuming furniture. Bookshelves lined the walls, each one stocked with everything except books – framed photos, knickknacks and a very impressive collection of snow globes.

Polly gestured proudly at the globes. "I've got snow globes from all over the world."

"Do you do a lot of traveling?" Carla asked.

"Not since Randall died," Polly replied. "But my friends bring them to me."

"You must have a lot of friends," Sam said as they stepped into the kitchen.

Polly returned to the stove, checking on several pots that were simmering. It smelled amazing.

"Hon, could you do me a favor and pour us all a

glass of tea?" Polly asked, pointing to a glass pitcher beside three empty glasses. "Ice is in the fridge door."

Carla, happy to have something to do, filled each glass with ice and tea. The sharp crack of ice shifting in the glasses made Sam instantly thirsty. Carla handed them their glasses, and Sam nearly drained his in one swallow.

"I hope you like brisket," Polly said. "This is my daddy's recipe and it's so good it'll make you wanna slap your mama."

She pointed to the kitchen table behind her. "Y'all have a seat. You're making me nervous standing around."

Sam and Carla complied quickly. Polly had a tone that made grown adults behave like well-trained children.

"I know I told you I was gonna make tortilla soup, but I feel tonight called for something more. I hope you don't mind. With all this awfulness going on, it's so nice to be able to take a break from the craziness of it all."

"It has been... an unfortunate series of events," Carla said. "Did you know Amy well?"

Polly paused mid-stir over the pot of simmering green beans, her gaze going distant before she slowly shook her head.

"That girl was such a sweetheart," she said, her voice softer. "I can't imagine a purer soul. I could barely wrap my head around her being in so much pain that she'd take her own life. Broke my heart clean in two."

She turned toward Carla.

"But thanks to you, I don't have to torture myself with that. Now... Good Lord, I shudder at the very thought of her being murdered. Especially not knowing how. I just pray she didn't suffer."

She topped off their tea. "Sebastion — I'm sorry, the sheriff — said you think she might've been poisoned?"

Carla shot Sam a look.

Why was the sheriff sharing information about the case with his sister-in-law?

Polly must have seen the curious look in Carla's eyes. "Don't worry. He tells me all kinds of things, but I can keep a secret."

Carla hesitated but realized her host was not going to let her leave the question unanswered.

"I think so," she answered carefully. "But until the toxicology tests come back, there's no way to know for certain."

Polly shook her whole body, as if to shake off the conversation.

"Good Lord, would you listen to me?" she said. "This is no kind of supper talk."

"It's kind of hard not to talk about it," Sam said. "And, trust me, it's not healthy to pretend it didn't happen."

He wasn't simply offering good advice; he was hoping to leave the door open for his own questions a little later.

"Well, tonight I need a break from it all," Polly said. "And so do the two of you. Now let's get this food on the table."

As they ate, the mood brightened, especially for Sam, who was far too focused on filling his stomach to dwell on murder.

"Miss Polly, this is amazing," Sam said between bites. "Is this how you got your husband?"

"Do you know I first laid eyes on Randall in the eighth grade?" Polly asked. "Hand to my heart, I knew he was gonna be mine right then and there."

"Eighth grade?" Carla asked.

"Oh, we didn't start dating for another two years," Polly replied, "but I had him on the hook the whole time. By the time I gave him a kiss, he was already putty in my hands."

She laughed to herself, then her smile fell.

"He died much too young. God rest his soul."

"Can I ask what happened?" Carla asked gently.

"Heart attack. Right where you're sitting. We were having dinner. Joking and laughing. Randall used to run a little farm supply store out back. He was telling me about this old boy, Garrett Belcher, who'd come looking for some fertilizer and was snot-slinging drunk. Middle of the day."

Polly started to laugh as she recounted the story. "Anyways, Randall was busy, so he pointed Garrett back to where the bags of feed were. Next thing he knew, he heard this God-awful commotion. He went running back there and all the feed had fallen off the shelf and was lying in a big pile on the ground. All Randall could see was Garrett's old boots sticking out, just kicking back and forth."

Polly was laughing so hard, she could barely speak. Sam and Carla were laughing, too, but mostly at Polly's contagious delight.

And then – without warning – she stopped and stared at the floor beside Carla's chair.

"Then he just fell over," she said quietly. "No words. No warning. Just gone. Like a switch flipped."

"Oh, Polly," Carla said, reaching out to squeeze her hand. "I'm so sorry."

Polly nodded in appreciation, swallowing her emotion. "I guess going out laughing is the best way to go."

"I wanna go in my sleep," Sam said.

Carla shot him a glare, letting him know that it wasn't time to compare death wishes.

"But laughing's good, too," Sam said, trying to salvage his comment.

Polly slapped the table. "Would you look at me? Here I go draggin' us back into the dark again. Let me get y'all some pecan pie."

"You hear that, Carla," Sam said. "Pecan pie. Carla here has very few weaknesses, but one of them, without a doubt, is pie."

"Your life's about to change, honey," Polly winked, getting up to go to the kitchen.

"Just a small slice, please," Carla yelled out to her.

"There's no such thing as a small slice in the Wheeler house," Polly yelled back.

She soon returned with two generous slices of pie, setting them in front of Sam and Carla.

"Oh my God, this smells incredible," Carla said, eyes widening.

"Well, hang on now," Polly said.

She scampered back to the kitchen and returned with her own slice of pie, along with a gallon of vanilla ice cream.

"It ain't pie without ice cream," she said, offering the tub to Carla.

Carla took it happily, nodding. "As much a part of the pie as the crust."

Polly turned to Sam. "Oh, I like her. She's a wise woman, Sam Lawson. I hope you mind her."

"You better believe I do," Sam said. "Or suffer the consequences."

"Tease all you want," Carla said, never looking up from her pie. "I'm in my happy place."

Carla took a bite and leaned back with a blissful moan.

"Mmmmm mmmm mmmm. Polly, this is heaven."

"I told you," Polly said proudly. "I don't lie. Especially when it comes to food."

They all turned their attention to their dessert and Sam soon joined his wife in praise.

"How did you learn to cook like this?" he asked.

"My momma taught me most everything, but believe it or not, I got the pie recipe from Randall."

"Well, here's to Randall," Sam said, raising his glass.

"I mean, I made it better," Polly said in total seriousness as they clinked glasses. "So, I guess I should get some of the credit. But it's pretty much his recipe."

"Is Randall where you got your love of real estate?" Sam asked.

The room fell stone-cold quiet. It was not the smooth transition Sam had hoped for.

Polly's eyes sharpened in a way that made Sam's spine itch.

"Why do you say that?" Polly asked.

"Oh, I didn't mean anything bad by it," Sam said quickly. "I've just been at the County Deeds office, where Amy worked. And I couldn't help but notice your name on a lot of deeds. You must own half the land in the county."

"It sounds richer on paper than it is," Polly said, her voice still flat as an ironed sheet.

"I believe you. Especially after everything else I heard," Sam said. "As you know, I've been asking around and I'm hearing some incredible stories about how you've helped so many people stay in their homes. It's astounding."

"Like I told you before, we take care of our own here," Polly said, pointing to Carla's half-eaten pie. "You better not leave a bite on that plate, hon. That's sacrilege."

"Oh, don't worry," Carla said. "I'm just catching my breath."

"It's just that... it must be tough to pay for all of that," Sam pressed, the only one interested in continuing the conversation. "I mean, between the loans and then covering all of those mortgages."

Polly's face reddened. "I shuffle things around to make it work. It's important to me, and it's what Randall would've wanted. The Lord always finds a way. Now while I understand your curiosity, it's not polite to talk money matters at the table. And, right now, us ladies are enjoying our pie. If you're done eating, why don't you do me a favor and clear the table?"

Sam recognized the dismissal and the warning simmering beneath it. He nodded.

"I can do that. I just wanted to tell you that I think what you're doing is incredibly admirable. That's all. Seriously. This town is lucky to have you."

Polly gave him a thin smile and a wink. "You're damn right about that."

41

———

WHILE SAM and Carla were navigating their dinner with Miss Polly, Constable Clyde Harlan was dealing with his own demons. He pulled into the crowded lot outside Diamond's, his eyes swollen from tears, nerves scraped raw, and body numbed by the whiskey he'd been drinking.

He didn't even like whiskey.

But it was the only thing that could quiet the grief that was gnawing through him. Hours of trudging through thickets and backroads had given him too much time to think. Too much time to remember his time with Amy... and what had eventually become of her. Time for his sorrow to recast itself as fury. And it was aimed squarely at Gus Booker.

He stumbled out of his vehicle, blinking at the neon sign flickering above the bar. Diamond's was not his kind of place, and the patrons were certainly not his kind of people. But grief can steer you on strange paths sometimes.

Wiping tears and snot from his face, Clyde unclipped his badge and gun belt. Even drunk, he respected the uniform too much to stain it with what he was about to do.

He was going in as Clyde Harlan, the man – not Clyde Harlan, Burdett County Constable.

He fought his way out of his constable shirt, falling twice as he tugged at the sleeves. Then he fumbled in his SUV and found a crumpled plaid shirt, which he yanked on crooked. He reached for the bottle of Jim Beam and took one last burning swallow before heading inside.

Inside, Diamond's was packed. Southern rock thundered from the jukebox, creating a blanket of music over the laughter, shouts, and clinking bottles. Clyde swung open the door like he had stepped into a saloon in the Wild West. But the music didn't stop and not a single head turned to take notice of him.

He scanned the room, trying to focus his blurred vision until he found who he was looking for.

Gus sat on a barstool, talking with the bartender.

Mandy stood by Gus's side, her arm hooked possessively through his.

Clyde's stomach rolled.

Her body's not even buried yet.

He staggered forward, fists clenched, rage boiling. As he got closer, Gus turned in his direction, as did Mandy and a few other patrons. Gus's grin faltered into confusion.

"Shit, Clyde. What the hell happened to you?"

"Dang," Mandy added, her nose pinched in disgust. "You get in a fight with a bobcat?"

Clyde frowned, reaching clumsily to his face. His fingers came away slick.

Blood.

He hadn't realized he was bleeding. For a moment, he forgot why he was there. Then it came crashing back.

"These..." Clyde gestured to the cuts and scratches on his cheeks, "are from the briars and thickets I've been walking through all day... trying to find out who killed your wife."

He aimed the last word directly at Mandy. She felt the blow and took a step back. But Gus didn't flinch.

"Oh yeah?" Gus asked. "And how's that going for you?"

"Like you give a damn," Clyde growled, taking a step forward.

Gus lifted a hand in warning. "Easy, big man. Looks like someone raided their momma's liquor cabinet."

The crowd that was growing behind Gus laughed. But Clyde slapped Gus's hand away.

"How dare you disrespect Amy like this," Clyde slurred. "She deserved better than you."

The words cracked like a pistol shot. Gus rose to his feet.

"You better watch your damn mouth."

But Clyde wasn't done.

"Movin' on already?" he sneered, tilting his head toward Mandy. "Was that the plan all along? Get rid of Amy to make room for another warm body?"

Mandy bristled. "Who the hell do you think you're talking to?"

Gus's expression hardened. "I think it's best you leave. Now."

But Clyde leaned in, trembling with drunken rage.

"You know something, Gus?" he said, voice low. "It makes you look guilty as sin."

Gus's jaw tightened. "I didn't kill her."

Clyde laughed bitterly. "Yeah? I don't believe you."

Gus shook his head, then leaned into Clyde. The two men were almost nose to nose.

"Well, it weren't me. But I know who it was."

The words hit the room like a dropped glass.

Clyde blinked. "What?"

"It was that creep, Skeeter," Gus said. "But you don't need to worry about any of that."

Clyde looked into Gus's eyes and then dismissed his claim. "You're full of shit," Clyde spat. "We both know you killed Amy."

The bluntness of the words was the spark needed to light the fuse. Gus's whole body went still.

"Say it again. I dare you."

"You heard me," Clyde slurred, louder this time. "You killed Amy."

Murmers rippled through the patrons. Gus clinched his fists and his neck tightened. "I'm gonna give you one chance to walk away."

Clyde responded by shoving Gus. It was weak – drunk and clumsy – but it was enough.

Gus shoved back, a solid, practiced bar-fight shove that sent Clyde sprawling onto the floor.

"I'm trying real hard not to break you," Gus said. "I want everyone here to be a witness to that."

By now, the crowd had circled the two men, eager for blood.

Clyde staggered up, shaking, jaw clenched. The shove had sobered him up just enough to sharpen his anger. Then he swung. His fist landed squarely on Gus's jaw, snapping the man's head to the side.

Gus turned back slowly, rubbing his lip. His smile was savage.

"She deserved better," Clyde growled.

"You deserve everything you're about to get," Gus sneered, low and lethal.

He shot a punch directly at Clyde's nose, then another. And another. Clyde's head snapped back with each blow, blood spurting anew. But he refused to fall. He swung back wildly, connecting with Gus's cheek, then his gut, forcing the bigger man to grunt.

But Gus was a seasoned brawler. Clyde was a grieving drunk.

Gus unleashed a barrage – hooks, jabs, an elbow toss that sent Clyde crashing into the bar. Glass shattered. Someone screamed. Gus grabbed Clyde by the shirt, spun him around, and slammed his head against the bar top.

Clyde dropped to the floor like a wet sack.

But Gus wasn't done.

He yanked Clyde up by the back of his flannel shirt and dragged him toward the door. The crowd hooted, cheering him on. Someone swung the door open, and Gus hauled Clyde outside, lifting him up to a standing position before punching him once more for good measure. The constable dropped into the dirt – sprawled, unconscious, bleeding.

"If you every accuse me like that again," Gus said, his voice ice-cold, "They'll be your final words."

He kicked dust into Clyde's face and turned back toward the door. The bar erupted in cheers, pulling Gus inside as if he were a conquering hero. Not one person looked back at Clyde Harlan – bleeding, wheezing, broken and alone in the dust.

42

———

"Well, that was something," Sam said.

"Are you talking about that pecan pie?" Carla asked, still salivating.

Sam and Carla were driving down the dark state highway back toward their motel on the other side of town. The overcast sky pressed low, and the thick pines arched over the road like they were conspiring to keep secrets, creating a dark tunnel that seemed to swallow up the truck's high beams. On these back roads, visibility was clearly on a "know-as-you-go" basis.

"That was good pie," Sam agreed. "But I'm talking about Polly. She's a force to be reckoned with."

"She's an insecure pussycat," Carla said.

"Insecure?" Sam laughed. "I've never seen a more confident woman in my life."

"Too confident," Carla replied. "She went out of her way to let us know she's queen bee of every hive she's ever strutted into."

"Exactly."

"That's exactly what insecure people do," Carla said. "You of all people know that."

She nudged her husband playfully. Sam smiled but shook his head.

"I don't see it," he said. "I think she just likes – real loudly likes – letting people know how good she is and how much good she does. Which makes me suspicious of it all."

"You're naturally suspicious. But I guess that's what makes you such a good — look out!"

Sam and Carla saw the dog in the road at the same time. Sam slammed the brakes and jerked the wheel as the dog leapt aside. The truck skidded sideways and came to a stop with two wheels kissing the ditch.

"Did you hit it?" Carla asked.

"I don't think so," Sam said, getting out of the truck.

He looked into the darkness, then reached behind his seat for a flashlight. By the time he turned back, Carla was beside him.

"I don't see anything," she said.

"I think it ran off that way," Sam said, pointing the flashlight at a patch of tall grass leading into the woods. They crept closer, bracing for what they might find. A sudden shuffle in the brush froze them where they stood.

Then an old hound stepped meekly out of the woods.

"Boone?" Sam asked, crouching.

The dog stepped toward him and began to lick his face.

"Does he look okay?" Carla asked.

Sam patted his body and examined his legs. "Seem's fine. Good boy."

"You called him Boone," Carla said.

"Looks like Boone. Hey, Boone."

The dog looked up at Sam and licked his face again.

"Where's Skeeter, boy?" Sam asked, standing and staring into the trees.

Boone turned, trotted toward the woods, then stopped and looked back, barking.

"That's not good," Sam said.

Sam and Carla followed the dog into woods that were so dark they made the highway look like a lit-up football stadium. Branches slapped at their arms and legs; briars grabbed at pant legs like little clawed creatures refusing to let go.

"Skeeter!" Sam yelled, again and again. Only tree frogs and crickets bothered to answer.

When the trees thinned, Boone broke into a run toward the creek up ahead. Sam immediately recognized Skeeter's tattered blue tarp drooping over a low branch. As he got closer, he saw more of Skeeter's things. But Boone ran past them all, bee-lining for the water. As Sam and Carla got closer, they saw why.

Skeeter lay at the shore's edge, face down in the creek.

"Shit," Sam yelled, running toward him.

He grabbed the old man and rolled him over. One of Skeeter's eyes had been blown out and there was a gaping, bloody crater at his right temple. Sam recognized the familiar wounds of someone who had shot themself in the head.

He swept the flashlight through the shallow water and spotted a pistol lying beneath the surface no more than a foot away. As Boone nudged his master's lifeless body with his nose, Carla dialed 9-1-1. Sam stood, staring down at Skeeter, the night suddenly heavy in his lungs.

Why would Skeeter kill himself? Sam wondered. *Had he become overcome with guilt? Or had he panicked because he thought he was about to get caught?*

Sam had been slow to believe Skeeter could have

been Amy's killer, but he had to admit this made him look more guilty.

Or is that exactly what this was intended to do?

"Don't touch anything," he said, more to himself than Carla. "Until the sheriff gets here and declares this a suicide, I'm treating it like a crime scene."

43

IT TOOK over an hour for the sheriff and a forensics team to respond, which gave Sam plenty of time to poke around on his own, being careful not to destroy the crime scene – not that the sheriff was going to treat it like one. From the look of the fire ring and the dead embers, Sam guessed Skeeter had set up camp here a couple of days earlier – probably right after the last time Sam had talked to him.

Sam replayed that frenzied conversation. Skeeter had definitely been battling some demons, but beneath that panic there had been some flat-out fear. Fear of something. Or someone. Maybe he'd seen something he shouldn't have. Maybe something tied to Amy's murder.

Another part of his previous conversation resurfaced. Skeeter had asked Sam for a gun. Sam had to assume that was because he didn't have one of his own. So where had he gotten the one he supposedly used to kill himself? Sam made a mental note to share that information with the sheriff. It would be easy enough to use the gun's serial number to track down its rightful owner. And Sam would definitely have some questions for whoever it was.

Because Sam wasn't so sure it was a suicide.

If he was a betting man — and he very much was — his money would be on the sheriff using Skeeter's death as an excuse to tie a great big bow around the case: Skeeter killed Amy, then killed himself. Investigation over. Case closed. What's for dinner?

Sam dialed Clyde's number again. Still no answer. *Where was he?*

He was supposed to have spent the day looking for Skeeter. While he clearly hadn't found him, maybe he found something else. At the very least, Sam needed to tell him to call off his search.

He was pulled from his thoughts by several flashlight beams slicing through the woods.

"Lawson?" the sheriff yelled. "You out there?"

"Over here," Sam yelled back, putting the ripped backpack he'd been examining back where he had found it.

He walked toward the tree line and turned his flashlight off and on to help guide them.

"Back here at a clearing by the creek," he yelled.

Boone barked loudly, echoing Sam's directions.

In less than a minute, the sheriff appeared out of the woods with two EMTs carrying a gurney. "Where is he?"

Sam pointed toward the creek. "Over there. Carla is getting some forensics."

"She's doing what?" the sheriff asked. "She's not our – damnit"

He stormed toward Skeeter's body. "Ma'am, could you step away from the body, please?"

Carla stayed crouched next to the body, calmly recording observations into her phone.

"Don't worry," she said to the sheriff. "I haven't disturbed anything. Just taking some pictures and recording some observational notes."

"You have no jurisdiction in this county," the sheriff reminded her. "You are just a civilian."

"I am," she said, standing. "A civilian who is also a trained medical examiner who just made your job easier. Unless R.J. came with you."

She looked back at the two paramedics. "No? I didn't think so. I'll share my notes and pictures with him in the morning so you can get a proper report, and R.J. can get his beauty sleep."

Sheriff Wheeler looked down at Skeeter's body. As he stared at the lifeless body, his anger softened to genuine grief. "Jesus, Skeeter. What'd you go and do?"

He crouched down and closed Skeeter's one good eye, letting out a long, deep sigh before standing again.

"I knew him before," the sheriff said quietly. "He was a good man. A really good man. I was proud to call him a friend. But then his family was taken from him and I had to watch him slip away. I didn't think it would ever lead to this. I should have seen the signs. Should have brought him in. Got him help. Something. I just wanted to believe the old Skeeter was still in there. And now..."

He pulled out his phone and took some pictures of the body.

"The gun's under water," Carla said softly. "Right over there."

The sheriff snapped some pictures of the gun.

"Eddie, you got evidence bags?" he yelled back to one of the paramedics.

Eddie brought over a small biohazard bag. "I got these."

"It'll have to do," the sheriff muttered.

He searched around the shore until he found a long, skinny stick he could run through the sunken gun's trigger guard to lift it out of the water.

"Be sure to find out whose gun that is," Sam said as the sheriff carefully placed the gun in the bag.

"No shit, Sherlock," the sheriff replied, examining the gun through the plastic. "Although that might not be so easy."

He held the bag toward Sam. "Looks like the serial number's been shaved off."

"Well, that's a little suspicious," Sam remarked.

"Not really. We find unmarked guns out in these woods all the time," the sheriff said. "Folks dump them off the highway. Illegal stuff mostly."

"You serious?" Sam asked. "Out here?"

"There's a lot of drugs running through this area," the sheriff replied. "Most of 'em coming up from Houston or over from Lafayette."

"And you get a lot of them?" Sam asked.

"Enough of 'em," the sheriff chuckled. "Or at least enough that it ain't much of a surprise when we find one."

He stepped back. "Well, not much more we can do here tonight," he said, motioning to the EMTs. "You think you boys can get him out of here okay?"

"You bet, Sheriff," Eddie replied as he and his partner laid out a body bag on dry land.

Sam started to protest. *No investigation of the area? No looking around for any sign this could be murder?* But Sam knew better than to argue. The sheriff would only dig his his heels in deeper.

The sheriff scratched his head. "I guess that puts a lid on all of this mess."

Here it comes, Sam thought. *The big, pretty bow.*

"I'm guessing Skeeter lured that poor girl to his house somehow, probably to help him with something. Then he killed her and, when we started looking for her, he tried to make it look like a suicide."

"But how did he kill her?" Carla asked.

"You said it yourself. Poison probably. Skeeter's lived out in these woods for years. There's all kinds of poisonous stuff out here and I guarantee you he knew it all."

"That's quite a big assumption, Sheriff," Sam said.

"It's what makes the most sense," the sheriff replied. "And then guilt, or fear of getting caught, just got the best of him."

He turned and looked at a skeptical Sam.

"Don't think I take delight in this. This is all gonna land on me," he said. "Folks been telling me forever to take care of Skeeter and I never did. Now I got two bodies on my hands because of it."

"I'm gonna go back with the body," Carla said to Sam.

Both the sheriff and Sam turned to her.

"I can help with the autopsy, and I don't want R.J. starting without me," she said.

"You're gonna have to get his permission for that," the sheriff said. "And I don't know how he's gonna feel about it."

"I'll deal with him," she said, confident as ever. "Four hands are better than two."

44

R.J. ARRIVED at the morgue around 1:30 a.m., still groggy from being yanked out of bed in the middle of the night but not surprised in the least to see Carla – already in a lab coat and standing over Skeeter's body.

"I don't mind your help, Doctor, but that doesn't give you free rein over my morgue."

"I meant no harm," Carla said. She spoke gently, hoping to lower the rising temperature in the room. "I had the EMTs unload the body. That's it."

Carla explained what R.J.. already knew – that she and Sam had found Skeeter's body, and she'd done a preliminary forensics scan of the scene before anyone else arrived.

"You and I both know they would stomp through

the area as soon as they got there," she said, handing her phone to R.J. so he could see the pictures she had taken. "And they did. I emailed all of these to you already."

She described the scene at the creek to him, reading from the notes she had already transcribed from her phone. R.J. listened as he put on his lab coat and performed a quick visual exam of Skeeter's body. As he turned Skeeter's head to inspect the entry wound, Carla added her commentary.

"Entrance wound right temple, contact or near-contact based on the powder tattooing. Exit wound left orbital socket."

"Pretty standard trajectory for a self-inflicted wound," R.J. said. "Seems pretty cut and dry to me."

"I'm not so certain," Carla said, anticipating R.J.'s reaction. "I think a full exam could tell us more."

R.J. sighed. He already knew from his previous dealings with Carla that she wasn't going to take no as an answer. And, truth be told, once he got over the humiliation of her taking over Amy's autopsy, he had enjoyed the thrill of making new discoveries that broke the case open.

"Alright, then," he shrugged. "Tell me what you're thinking."

Carla dove in immediately. "I noticed the soot

pattern around the entry wound is heavy but irregular. If he held the gun himself, I'd expect more consistent contact marks. Also, the trajectory angle seems to be slightly downward. Maybe fifteen degrees."

"There's a lot of conjecture in all of those statements," R.J. said. "Let's try to stick with the facts."

Carla nodded, willing to play by R.J.'s rules. She was confident the facts would support her so-called assumptions.

"I also checked his hands," she said, speaking of gunshot residue.

"You said his hands were submerged when you found him," R.J. replied. "Water'll wash away any gunshot residue over time."

"True. But I don't see any blowback in the web of his thumb. That would be fairly common after firing a pistol."

"If what you're getting at is that someone else shot Skeeter, you've got nothing to support that," R.J. said, already weary of Carla's exam. "I don't see any signs of struggle. No scratch marks. No pre-mortem bruising."

"You're right," Carla conceded. "My observations are more about what I think did NOT happen."

"'Think' being a key word there, Mrs. Lawson."

"Dr. Lawson," she corrected, steady as a fence post. "And I'd like to examine his brain."

The request took R.J. by surprise.

"I don't think we need to get crazy here," he said.

"Look, this is a small community," Carla said, prepared for this argument. "Even if his cause of death seems obvious to you and me, people are gonna talk. I know. I live in a small town, too. The more thorough we can be, the less likely people are going to question your conclusions. It only helps you."

"You saying we're gonna cut this man's skull open to help cover my ass?" R.J. asked.

"He's already dead, sir. But it's your call."

R.J. thought about it and finally nodded. "Let's get prepped."

After removing, examining and bagging Skeeter's clothing, they prepared for post-mortem surgery. Using a scalpel and oscillating saw, they carefully removed the skull cap, exposing the bullet path.

"Bullet track goes from right to left, slightly back to front, and at a downward angle," R.J. said as he examined the damaged brain tissue. "Like you said, about fifteen degrees."

"So that reinforces my theory," Carla said. "It's an awkward angle for a self-inflicted wound."

She stood back and pretended to hold a gun to her temple. "If you're going to shoot yourself, you're typically going to shoot at a ninety-degree angle. Or maybe slightly up."

She demonstrated with her hands, tracing a bullet path from the position of the imaginary gun.

"For the trajectory to go from back to front at a downward angle, he would have had to position the gun like so."

She lifted her arm up and back to put the imaginary gun at the right angle. "That's not a natural position."

"He could have moved as he fired," R.J. countered.

"That would sure be an odd way to absorb a recoil," Carla replied. "And the entry wounds don't suggest any movement. Also, when we removed his clothing, I noticed something else."

She pointed to small contusions and bruises on his knees.

"These look to be pre-mortem, but they're fresh. Consistent with someone forced to his knees."

R.J. shook his head and chuckled. "You're reaching. It's also consistent with a drunk who stumbled. Or a person who dropped to their knees before taking their life."

"I also examined the gun while I was waiting for you," Carla said.

R.J. shook his head, clearly annoyed.

"There were no prints," Carla said.

"The gun was submerged," R.J. growled, clearly agitated now.

"But for less than twelve hours," Carla replied.

"Water doesn't wash away prints that quickly. There should still be some prints at least - even if slightly contaminated. But this gun was wiped clean. Or he was wearing gloves."

"Except he was not wearing gloves when his body was found," R.J. replied with a nod, understanding Carla's logic. "So, he would have had to remove them after he shot himself. Highly unlikely if not impossible."

"And none were found in the area"

R.J. nodded. He was beginning to get caught up in the investigation. He turned his gaze to Skeeter's gunshot wound.

"Look. I've been doing this a long time," he said calmly. "And I have had more than my share of suicides. Happens more than you think out here. Man runs out of options, walks down to the creek and ends it. They all look a lot like this."

Carla started to protest but R.J. held up his hand, so she'd let him finish.

"But there are too many unanswered questions. The trajectory. The wiped gun. No blowback. Any one of those, I could chalk up to chance. But all three? Something ain't right."

Carla nodded. Relieved to have R.J. on board.

"We should run ballistics. Get a toxicology report," she suggested excitedly.

"I'll mark the preliminary report as 'pending further investigation,'" R.J. said. "Keep it open so it requires a further investigation."

He looked at Carla and grinned. "Good detective work, doctor."

"Same to you," Carla smiled back.

45

———

Sam opened his eyes at the sound of the approaching vehicle. Having been up most of the night, he had attempted to catch a little shuteye in his truck while waiting for the sheriff to show up at his office. He squinted at his watch, coaxing the blur into numbers. It was 1:04 in the afternoon.

Climbing out of his truck, he intercepted the sheriff before either of them reached the door.

"Hey there, Sheriff," he croaked, still groggy.

The sheriff looked at him and let his shoulders sag in disappointment. "Sam. What a surprise."

"Getting a late start on the day, huh?" Sam grinned.

"At least I'm awake now," the sheriff muttered. "It was a long night. And Skeeter ain't no more dead now than he was a few hours ago."

He walked into the building, not bothering to hold the door for Sam and bee-lined it for the coffee pot. Sam followed and stood next to the sheriff as he poured himself a cup.

"I can't vouch for how long this has been sitting here," the sheriff grumbled, carrying his coffee cup to his office.

"As long as it's hot and has caffeine in it," Sam said, pouring his own cup and shuffling quickly to catch up to the sheriff.

He lingered in the doorway as the sheriff settled behind his desk, flipping through a scattering of Post-it Notes that had been affixed all over his desk. He picked up one and read it as he turned his computer on.

"Interesting way to get notes," Sam commented.

"Keeps 'em from flying all over the place until I read them," the sheriff replied.

He crumpled a Post-it Note and dropped it on the desk. As he waited for the computer to start up, he read the other notes, one at a time, each getting the same treatment: read, grunt, crumple, drop.

Seeing that the sheriff was not in a particularly talkative mood, Sam decided to hold his questions. He sipped his coffee and winced.

"Jesus, this is awful," he grimaced.

"I warned ya," the sheriff said.

Sam took the opening and sat down across from the

sheriff. "You warned it could be *old*. This is just outright nasty."

"You're welcome to go get your own somewhere else," the sheriff said, crumpling another note.

He turned to the computer, opened an email, and clicked the link to see the coroner's report.

"I'm guessing you already saw this," the sheriff said.

"I got the Reader's Digest version."

The sheriff skimmed the report.

"Damnit, R.J.," he muttered, shaking his head.

"Not as conclusive as you'd hoped?" Sam asked.

"This has got your wife's fingerprints all over it," the sheriff growled.

"Looks like it's got your coroner's signature at the bottom there," Sam said.

"I already spoke to him," the sheriff said. "Your wife is a bad influence."

"Those pesky facts," Sam teased

"The facts don't conclude anything."

"That's kinda the point, right? That's literally what 'pending further investigation' means."

The sheriff leaned across his desk and stared Sam down.

"You were there," he said. "There's not much more to investigate."

"Not much more at the scene of the crime," Sam said. "I'll give you that."

"There's no proof any *crime* was committed," the sheriff said.

Sam leaned forward. "We're thinking the same thing, whether you want to admit it or not. Skeeter may have seen something. He was a loose end. The evidence supports that theory as much as – if not more than – he killed himself out of guilt."

"And who do you suppose that someone was?" the sheriff asked.

"That's what needs further investigating."

The sheriff narrowed his eyes. "Weren't you hired to look into Amy's disappearance? Seems like that question has been answered."

Sam could hear the threat in his tone.

"What are you getting at, Sheriff?"

"Far as I know, nobody hired you for any murder investigation. Am I right?"

"Judy Duncan hired me to find out what happened to her sister," Sam said. "I think finding her killer is part of that."

"I don't know if she'd agree with that," the sheriff said. "Because the way I see it, you're just some out-of-towner P.I. trying to take advantage of a situation to milk a grieving, mentally unstable relative out of more money."

"I don't think Judy Duncan would agree with that," Sam said.

"I think she would," the sheriff replied. "In fact, that's pretty much exactly what she told me."

Sam straightened, stunned.

"She did not," he said.

"Why don't you give her a call? Hell, I'll call her for you."

The sheriff dialed and put the phone on speaker.

"Sheriff?" Judy answered.

"Judy. Sheriff Wheeler here. Do you mind repeating what you told me about your concerns with Sam Lawson?"

There was a pause on the other end. "That he's prolonging the investigation so he can take my money?" Her voice trembled slightly, unsure.

The sheriff smiled at Sam.

"Miss Duncan, I promise that's not true," Sam said.

There was another pause. "Is that you, Mr. Lawson?"

"It is. And I swear to you; I am not trying to take advantage of you. I won't even charge you for this."

"Judy, did you sign a contract with Mr. Lawson?" the sheriff asked. "If you did, here's a word of advice. I wouldn't take him at his word. He could take you to court with that document."

"I won't," Sam said. "You can rip it up. I'll write a new contract."

"I don't know," Judy stammered. Sam could hear a bit of panic in her voice.

"Judy, it's okay. You can tell him what you told me. That he's just making things worse."

Sam protested. "I'm trying to find out what really happened to your sister."

There was a hesitation on the other end. "I appreciate all you've done, Mr. Lawson. But I can't keep paying you."

It sounded rehearsed. Or like she was reading it. The sheriff must have got in her head. Someone like Judy could be easily steered, especially if it involved something that sounded like a conspiracy.

"I told you – you don't have to pay me."

"I think we should let the sheriff handle it from here," she replied. "I trust him. I'll pay you for all the time you've put in so far, but... please stop now. I have to go."

And with that, she hung up.

Sam looked up at the sheriff. "What'd you say to her?"

"Did you hear me put any words into her mouth?"

"You talked to her already," Sam said. "Did you lie to her? Threaten her?"

The sheriff clenched his jaw. "I think it is in your best interest to follow your client's advice. Time you head on home, Mr. Lawson."

Sam shot up, pushing his chair back. "Are you threatening me now?"

"Thank you for all of your help," the sheriff said, his glare contradicting his words. "But she's right. I can handle it from here. I'll call in the Texas Rangers. Conduct a full investigation. It's time you let official law enforcement do our job."

Sam stared him down, his mind whirring to think of something to do but coming up empty. He lowered his gaze – just enough to catch a name on one of the crumpled Post-its. He straightened slowly, masking what he had noticed.

"Alright. You win," he said. "I'll get Carla, and we'll leave. Don't hesitate to call if you need anything. A statement. A description. Whatever."

The sheriff stood and shook Sam's hand. "I will do that, but don't hold your breath."

Sam had barely settled into his truck before calling Carla. It rang several times before she answered, barely awake.

"Sam, I'm trying to get a little sleep," she croaked.

"You are so sexy when you're half-asleep," Sam teased.

"That may be one of the creepiest things you've ever said," she replied.

"Really? I'm gonna have to up my game," Sam

quipped. "Listen, I need you to meet me at the County Courthouse ASAP."

"Why?"

Before he could answer, a text came through from Clyde.

"How does he keep doing this?" Sam muttered, further confusing Carla. He opened the message, and as he read it, his face drained of color.

"Holy shit."

"Sam. What's going on?" Carla asked.

"Call me when you're on the way to the courthouse. I'll explain everything."

"What are you going to do?"

"I need to go see Clyde. He's in the hospital."

46

As he drove to the hospital, Sam stayed on the phone with Carla, filling her in on his talk with the sheriff and Judy – and what he'd noticed on the Post-its.

"You think the sheriff is involved?" she asked. "Maybe he's just territorial. We both are kind of invading jurisdictions here."

"Honestly, I don't know what to think. Or who to be looking at," Sam admitted. "Gus is still at the top of the list. Using a bar as your alibi isn't exactly airtight. And then there's that Toby guy out by the creek. And creepy Walter definitely had an unhealthy obsession with Amy."

He sighed, not wanting to say the next sentence aloud.

"Plus, I hate to say it, but we don't know where

Clyde was last night. Just that he wound up in the hospital."

"You forgot about the other obvious one," Carla said. "That the sheriff's theory is right and Skeeter did it."

"Neither one of us believes that's true," Sam said.

"Doesn't mean it's not," Carla replied.

"And then there's Polly's weird land grab," Sam continued. "I still think Amy stumbled on to something we haven't found yet."

"I'm almost at the County Court. I'm guessing that's why I'm here?"

Sam stepped into Clyde's hospital room and nodded at the old man in the first bed. He walked past the cloth partition to Clyde's side – and winced at what he saw.

A thick bandage was wrapped around most of Clyde's head, but it still barely covered his bruised, swollen eye and mottled cheek. Clyde was so swollen, he could barely open his eyes. And he was covered in so many cuts and bruises it looked like he'd taken a slow tumble through a wood chipper. Both arms were scraped and bruised. His left arm was in a sling; his right was tethered to an IV feeding Clyde what Sam could only assume was some heavy-duty pain medication.

"What in the holy hell happened to you?" Sam asked.

"I... uhm... did something stupid," Clyde mumbled, the swelling making it hard for him to open his mouth.

"Did you jump in front of a moving bus?" Sam said, marveling at Clyde's injuries. "Jump off a building?"

"Picked a fight with Gus Booker."

"Did he have a baseball bat or something?"

Clyde ignored that. "I heard about Skeeter."

"Yeah, I take it you never found him," Sam said, plopping down in the chair next to Clyde's bed. "But I think somebody did. When did this happen?"

Clyde managed to mumble out enough of his story for Sam to get the high points. Clyde had spent the day and evening looking for Skeeter in all the usual places, plus a handful of unlikely ones. Hours alone gave him plenty of time to stew and, next thing he knew, he'd picked up a bottle of whiskey, drowned in it, and then marched into Diamond's to confront Gus.

"I know he did it," Clyde said. "It has to be him."

"So, you decided to go full cowboy," Sam said, shaking his head.

Clyde's version of the fight gave himself far too much credit, but the ending was the same: Clyde crumpled in a heap outside the bar, stomped into unconsciousness.

"Cleaning crew found me this morning."

Sam blinked. "Wait. You're telling me that everyone that left the bar that night just stepped right over you? They seriously do not like you."

"They hate the badge," Clyde muttered. "I'm The Man to them. Comes with the job."

"Oh, don't sell yourself short. They don't like *you*. As a person. At all."

Clyde tried leaning forward toward his cup. Sam picked it up and guided the straw to Clyde's busted lips.

"So, what's our plan?" Clyde asked.

"Your plan is to lay here and soak up those pain killers, my friend."

He filled Clyde in on the autopsy results – and how it did not look like a suicide. He also told him how the sheriff had clearly strong-armed Judy Duncan into firing him.

"So, what's the plan?" Clyde repeated the question, knowing Sam was not going to just walk away. "Are we gonna get Gus?"

Sam smirked. "I don't think Gus is our man. But I've got a hunch. It's a long shot, but it's about time for a Hail Mary."

He told Clyde about the name he'd seen on the

crumpled Post-it – and the theory that had been gnawing at him. Clyde heard him out.

"You're not kidding about a long shot," he said.

"It's all we got right now," Sam answered.

"Alright. I'll help," Clyde said, attempting to sit up. "My clothes are up in that bureau there."

"Hold on, Kemosabe," Sam said, standing and gently pushing Clyde back down. "You blew your chance to help. In your condition, you'd be more of a liability than anything."

Clyde started to argue but Sam raised his hand to stop him.

"Actually," Sam said. "There may be something you can do."

47

———

SAM HID his truck down the road, tucking it behind a thick clump of wild elderberry bushes, and waited. As he'd hoped, the gold Cadillac rolled out of the driveway and headed toward Burdett. He gave it a few extra minutes – enough cushion to make sure she didn't double back – then slipped out of his truck and cut through a patch of woods toward Polly Wheeler's house.

Clyde had called Polly, pretending to be looking for the sheriff. Sam knew the local do-gooder wouldn't be able to resist the chance to help a person in need – especially in such a public place like a hospital. Even if her visit was short, it would buy him a solid thirty minutes to snoop around.

If he only knew what it was he was looking for.

He avoided the front door, remembering Polly's video doorbell that was most likely motion activated. He prayed that was the extent of her home protection.

He remembered a small side door that opened into the kitchen and decided to try his luck there. No cameras. No motion lights. And it was unlocked.

This might be easier than I thought.

Sam eased the door open, hoping the house was empty.

"Hello?" he called out softly, ready to claim he was just popping in to say goodbye if he got caught. But there was no answer.

Sam headed to the living area, where he had noticed an antique slant-top desk the night before. It reminded him of the one his grandmother had in her home. Sam had always loved the way the slant front panel folded out to create a writing desk, revealing several small drawers and slots for writing utensils and stationery. It had been a childhood treasure chest and Sam felt a flutter of that same boyhood thrill as he lowered the polished mahogany lid and swung out the support bars.

Like his grandmother's bureau, the mail slots were filled with blank envelopes, and the tiny drawers were packed with pens, stamps, rubber bands and paper clips. Nothing even close to incriminating.

He carefully closed the bureau lid and opened the

large drawers underneath, finding nothing but linens, some polished silverware and enough doilies to wallpaper the entire house. But nothing of interest.

He closed the drawers and scanned the room, thinking of where people would hide things they didn't want found.

Everyone hides things in their bedroom, he thought. *It's the one place in the house even the nosiest neighbors tend to respect.*

But the bedroom turned up nothing of interest. Just a few things in Polly's underwear drawer Sam wished he could unsee. But nothing criminal.

Since Sam had started his investigation of Amy's disappearance, something about Polly's inherited properties had kept needling him. It all seemed to be on the up and up, even charitable. But what was she doing with all that land once all the survivors were gone? She wasn't renting it. Wasn't selling it. Just collecting it like charms on a bracelet. Polly seemed too smart for that. There was something he was missing.

That's why he'd sent Carla to the courthouse to team up with Walter again – even if having one of his prime suspects help with the investigation made him itch.

Sam spent the next half hour searching room to room until he reached the final door in the hallway.

It was locked.

Non-plussed, Sam pulled out the lock-picking kit he carried in his back pocket the way some men carry handkerchiefs. Two twists and one click later, the lock yielded and he opened the door.

Before Sam could step inside, his phone pinged. It was a text from Clyde.

SHE'S ON HER WAY BACK.

Sam knew he only had a few minutes and had to act fast. He looked around. The room was chaos – spare furniture, teetering piles of storage boxes, a couple of file cabinets, and a desk buried back in the far corner. From the lamp sitting next to it and the computer monitor on top of it, it was clearly a working office.

Sam pushed the chair aside and dropped to his knees to try the drawers. As he expected, they were all locked, but it only took a few seconds for Sam to release the flimsy mechanism, and he slid open the drawer. It was filled with file folders of bank records and credit card statements. Polly apparently was a big believer in saving her paperwork. He quickly rifled through it, but nothing stood out as suspicious at all. The bank balances were modest at best, and her expenses were boring – nothing that whispered of wrongdoing.

Still, Sam had looked through enough desk drawers to know they often lied. He carefully removed all the files and set them beside him, then he pressed at the corners of the drawer bottom. As expected, a false bottom popped up. Underneath it was a small, leather-bound notebook.

Sam's heart thudded.

Could this be Amy's missing journal? The smoking gun he'd been chasing?

But Sam remembered Walter saying Amy's journal was pink. This one was black. Also, one look at the handwriting, plus notes about Randall, told him this journal must belong to Polly.

Sam flipped through its pages. There were personal notes, reminders, even a recipe or two. But nothing worth hiding. Then a page of numbers flipped by. Sam thumbed back to the page. It was a ledger of sorts.

The first column was a list of names – some he recognized from the deed transfers. The second column contained dollar amounts. Some had been crossed out and some circled. Then there was a third column that held other names, usually just a first name, and some of them were crossed out and circled similarly.

One entry snagged his eye like a fishhook.

Efrem Garrett – $25,000, crossed out – Lila Mae, circled.

What the hell does that mean?

He snapped a few pictures of the ledger pages with his phone and sent them to Carla with a quick explanation. Then he pulled out a document that had sat underneath the journal. As he skimmed it, his breath caught.

Holy hell, now it all makes sense.

He took a picture of the document and then placed it back at the bottom of the drawer. As he sat the ledger on top of it, he heard a vehicle pull into the driveway.

48

––––––––

CARLA PULLED up a chair next to Walter as he typed his login information into the computer.

"I'm still not clear on what we're looking for," he said.

"I'm not too sure either," Carla replied. "Sam just wanted us to cross-check against the list we put together."

She straightened out the folded piece of paper next to the computer's keypad.

"I barely know more than you," she continued. "He didn't even tell me about this until I was almost in the parking lot. I had to go all the way back to our motel room to get the list."

"Sam doesn't strike me as much of a planner,"

Walter remarked, eyes glued to the screen. "Okay. I'm in. What are we cross-referencing?

Carla pointed to the paper. "These are all the people who died and left their property to Polly. First thing we need to do is see how each of them died."

"I don't have to look up half of these," Walter said. "It's a small town. I know how they died."

"Humor me," Carla said. "This might be a wild goose chase, but Sam's hoping we'll find something."

After thirty minutes of digging through death certificates, they'd nearly finished the list.

"Are you seeing anything I'm not?" Walter asked. "Even the ones that weren't natural causes are all pretty standard stuff. Heart attacks. Pneumonia. Alzheimer's complications. Respiratory failure."

"One car accident," Carla pointed out.

"And the poultry farm fire," Walter added. "That killed three men, but only one of them was on our list – and the fire was due to faulty wiring."

"Right now, let's gather all the data," Carla said, slipping into her scientific mode. "We'll save any conclusions for later."

Her phone pinged – it was a text from Sam. She

opened it to see the picture of the ledger notes he had taken.

"Hang on. Sam sent something."

She studied the picture, then handed her phone to Walter.

"Looks a lot like our list," Walter said. "Where'd he get it?"

"He didn't say," Carla replied, studying the columns. "Just that he wanted us to see if we could make sense of it."

She compared the photo list to their paper list, and something clicked. She double-checked it quickly.

"All of the names with the lines through them are people who have died. But what are the circles for? How did those people die?"

Walter compared the picture to their list. "Respiratory failure. Pneumonia. Heart attack. Car accident. Fire. Kidney failure. Cancer."

"What about this third column? It looks like a list of the surviving spouses. Some of them have been crossed out."

Walter took the first crossed-out name in the third column and entered it into his database. "Deceased. Respiratory failure."

Carla scribbled that on the list.

"Try a circled name," she said.

Walter entered the first person's name. "Morgan Ketchum. I know she's still alive."

"Is she healthy?" Carla asked.

A realization hit Walter. "No. She's been really sick. I think she's in the hospital."

"Let me guess. Respiratory issues. What about this name?"

"Lila Mae Garrett," Walter said as he typed it. "She used to be my teacher. I'd have heard if she passed. Yep. Still alive."

"Do you know if she's sick?"

"That I couldn't tell you," Walter said. "I can't access medical records."

Carla tapped the list, thinking. "Let's run through all the circled names. Tell me what you know about any of them."

Walter took the phone and zoomed in on the survivor column, scrolling through to each circled name without a strike through it. "She's been real sick for a while... he's in hospice... I don't know this person... Ruby Gorman. I saw her at the Walmart the other day and she did not look good. Coughing nonstop."

Carla scribbled notes on the list next to each person Walter named. When he'd finished, they stared at the page.

"Beginning to look a little suspicious yet?" Carla asked.

"When you see it all together like this, something's sure not right," Walter replied.

"Can you pull up all the death certificates from the past nine months?" Carla asked, following a hunch.

Walter typed a command and a list appeared on the monitor. "I'd have to click on each one to get details."

"That's okay. All I need are the names."

Carla checked the list against the names on Sam's picture.

"Other than two people, every single name on that list is either someone who willed property to Polly Wheeler or the surviving spouse of that person."

"Are you saying Miss Polly's involved in this?" Walter asked. "How is she causing people to have heart attacks? Or cancer? That doesn't make any sense."

"Not yet," Carla said. "But I'm starting to get an idea what we're looking for."

49

SAM SHOVED the false bottom back in place and scrambled to put all the files back. As car doors shut and footsteps walked toward the house, he slipped out of the room to the rear of the house. He carefully eased the back door closed just as the front door opened, timing the click of the door to synchronize with the front door shutting. Knowing he couldn't circle around the side of the house without being seen through the windows, Sam darted across the yard to the tractor shed he'd seen the night before.

Luckily, the shed door was unlocked. He slipped inside and peered back toward the house through a sliver in the doorway. Satisfied he hadn't been spotted, he shut the door all the way and turned, silently praying he wouldn't be staring nose-to-nose with a bull.

Much to Sam's relief, the shed was livestock-free. Instead, it was crammed floor to rafters with all sorts of agricultural supplies. The air was filled with the scent of dust and chemicals thick enough to taste as Sam made his way to a large workbench in the back. Lined up next to it were several empty milk jugs – the gallon-size, grocery-store kind. On the table, there was a funnel and a 25-gallon container of something that smelled offensively like garlic. Sam turned the container around to read its label.

MALATHION 5EC INSECTICIDE

He noticed watermarks around the container and a yellowish fluid still puddled in the funnel. The acrid garlic stink clung to the air, and the wet sheen on the bench suggested someone had been using the funnel to transfer the chemical recently – very recently.

What was Polly doing with all this pesticide? For all he knew, she was using it the way it was intended, but why pour it into milk jugs? Something about it seemed off. And that large warning at the bottom of the container didn't help:

WARNING: POISON. KEEP OUT OF REACH OF CHILDREN

If his hunch was right, this could be the missing piece of the puzzle. Sam snapped a quick picture and sent it to Carla. He ventured deeper into the shed, past stacked bags of fertilizer and other farm supplies. Aside from the freshly used workbench, the rest of the shed looked untouched – except for a red metal toolbox pushed against the back wall. While everything else was carpeted in a thick layer of red dust, the toolbox had fresh hand marks on it. And while there was nothing suspicious about someone using a toolbox, finding it recently used but hidden away in the back of the shed certainly was.

Sam knelt and released the two metal toggle latches, opening the lid. The top tray held standard tools – a hammer, some screwdrivers, a utility knife – but when Sam removed the top tray and when he saw what was underneath, his breath caught in his throat.

He pulled out a small but thick pocket journal with a pink leather cover.

Amy's journal.

Sam thumbed through the pages. Aside from a few personal entries, it was filled with names, dollar amounts, and addresses. Sam immediately recognized some of the names from Polly's ledger.

Is this what Amy had discovered that got her killed?

"Put your hands up."

The voice hit Sam like a cattle prod. He nearly pitched forward, but steadied himself on the toolbox, using the opportunity to place the journal back inside of it. Then he slowly raised his hands.

"Lock your fingers behind your head and turn around. Slowly."

Sam recognized the voice. He let out a sigh and turned to face the sheriff, his handgun aimed directly at Sam.

50

———

THE SHERIFF ESCORTED Sam back into Polly's kitchen and motioned for him to sit down at the table. He took a seat across from him and sat his Glock 19 on the table, hand still wrapped around the grip, finger resting a whisper too close to the trigger, barrel pointed directly at Sam.

"I told you to leave well enough alone," the sheriff said.

"I'm not really good at taking hints," Sam said. "Ask my wife. She thinks I'm an idiot."

"I'd have to agree with her," Polly said, entering the room. "You've been going through my things, Mr. Lawson."

"Breaking and entering," the sheriff said.

"The door was unlocked," said Sam. "So technically speaking, that's only trespassing."

"Says you," Miss Polly countered. "I always lock my doors. Always."

"That's why you needed these," the sheriff said, tossing Sam's lock-picking kit on the table. "Found 'em in his back pocket. A man don't need one of these if he don't plan on using it."

Polly slammed her black leather journal – the one from the hidden drawer – on the table in front of Sam. "I don't appreciate you digging through my personal files."

"I don't know what you're talking about or what that even is," Sam said, playing dumb.

"Don't play me the fool, Mr. Lawson," Polly said. "You left the drawer open. And this journal was facedown. I always place it face-up. Always. That way, I know if anybody's been prying."

Sam tried to keep a blank expression on his face, but he was kicking himself for being so sloppy.

"Found him back in the shed. Going through the toolbox," the sheriff said.

Polly planted her hands on her hips, hovering over Sam like a judge deciding the prison sentence for the defendant.

"So, you saw the other journal," she finally said.

"Not if you tell me I didn't," Sam offered.

"I found that out in the woods," she said. "Near where Skeeter camped. But I knew that would make him look guilty, so I hid it."

Sam laughed and shook his head. "That's quite gracious of you."

"I'm a very gracious woman, Sam Lawson. Until I'm crossed."

She turned and opened the fridge and pulled out a glass bowl covered in Saran Wrap. She ladled the contents into a pot sitting on the stove.

"You like beef stew?" she asked. "I'm gonna heat you up some beef stew."

"Thanks, but I'm not that hungry," Sam replied.

"I don't understand why you feel the need to persecute me," Polly said, stirring. "I break my back taking care of my community, making sure folks don't lose their property."

"Until they die," Sam added. "Then it's yours. Am I right?"

"Better it come to me than the bank," Polly said.

"Right," Sam said. "Can't trust a bank. They'd just sell the property for fair market value and call it a day."

Polly shook her head. "I'm doing a service. I'm helping my people. Why do you insist on finding fault with that."

"At first, I couldn't," Sam said. "I beat myself up for being so cynical. But I kept coming back to Amy and how she'd been looking into all those property deeds right before she died. And I kept wondering, what did she find that was worth killing her over?"

"Maybe you've got too active of an imagination," the sheriff commented.

Sam nodded. "Oh, I have definitely been accused of that more than once. And, honestly, I was having a hard time putting the pieces of this puzzle together. It just struck me as strange that all these people agreed to will their land to you and then they die."

"Time takes us all sooner or later," Polly replied.

"True. Still, it was rubbing me the wrong way. I couldn't figure out what you had to gain from it. You weren't selling the land, and it wasn't even worth that much. That's why the bank never made a stink about it."

"Not everything is about money, Mr. Lawson. Sometimes it's about doing what is right."

Sam chuckled. "That is very true. Just not in this case." He tapped the black ledger in front of him. "I admit. I did see this ledger. I also saw the document underneath it. Some sort of contract between you and..." He snapped his fingers to help him recall the name. "Southern Sun Properties. Is that it? Don't they own a bunch of luxury hotels and stuff?"

Sam could see Polly's face redden before she turned to add salt and pepper to the stew.

"I admit. I don't know every inch of this town," Sam continued. "But from what I could tell, it looked like you agreed to sell them that whole stretch of land out there at Cypress Meadows. Where all those homes are. Property that's been willed to you. I'm pretty sure I saw it came with a pretty big payday, too. Problem is, you got a lot of survivors still living in those homes."

Polly shot a venomous glare at Sam. "I never heard a fool spit so much nonsense in my life."

"Again, something I've heard many times," Sam said. "But see, I noticed another detail in that contract. It expires in six months. You had a deadline. And that put you in a bad position. You couldn't just start buying out property openly. People would catch on. Prices would go up. And if you started kicking people out, that would bring more attention to what was going on. Like you said, time takes us all. Problem was, you were running out of time. You needed to speed things up. Maybe with that pesticide I saw in your shed."

Polly stiffened for a second.

"Polly, you don't gotta say nothing," the sheriff said.

"And you've been helping her," Sam said to the sheriff. "Covering up crimes. Rushing autopsies. Stonewalling me. I just thought you were lazy. But you were protecting her."

The sheriff lifted the handgun up, tightening his grip.

"You best watch your mouth, son."

His voice was tough, but Sam saw a flicker of guilt in his eyes. He turned to see Polly open a cabinet and grab a milk jug similar to the ones he had seen in the shed. She poured some of the yellow liquid into the stew.

"I'm betting that Amy started seeing a pattern between the wills and the deaths in this town," Sam said.

He kept his eyes trained on the sheriff. "And I'm guessing she brought her concerns to you. Because you're the sheriff. The county's protector. She trusted you."

The sheriff's eyes narrowed slightly, letting Sam know his words had hit their targets.

"But you told Miss Polly, and she had you abduct Amy at the courthouse that night and bring her here. How am I doing?"

"He can't prove any of that," Polly said, noticing the flicker of guilt in the sheriff's eyes.

"Is this how you killed Amy?" Sam asked. "Right here at this table? Did you watch her die, Sheriff? Did you just sit here as your sister-in-law poisoned an innocent woman?"

The sheriff looked down. Sam could tell that hearing it all said out loud as an accusation cut through all the rationalizations the sheriff had concocted to make peace with what he had been involved with. Sam saw the sheriff's guilt as a crack in this partnership that could work in his favor. He decided to push it further.

"So, what'd you do? Bury her out back? That would explain the blue tarp fragments found in her hair. You rolled her up in a tarp and buried her... I'm guessing somewhere in the barn out there."

"He's reaching, Sebastian. Ignore him."

"And then, after the shoe was found and you saw that I wasn't buying the whole 'ran away from home' story, you dug up her body and took it to Skeeter's basement, where you staged a suicide by hanging."

Sam fixed his accusations on the sheriff but couldn't help but notice Polly ladling some of the stew into a bowl.

"You were counting on R.J. to do his usual half-assed autopsy based on what you told him. But you weren't counting on my wife forcing a second examination. You started scrambling. So, you tried to frame Skeeter for Amy's murder. Although you have to admit, you did a pretty sloppy job of it."

The sheriff had yet to look up but now he was shaking his head. If they were in an interrogation room, Sam would know he was about to crack. But Sam was not in the position of power. He had a gun pointed at him and a crazy lady was making him a bowl of poison.

She placed the bowl in front of Sam and handed him a large spoon.

"Time for you to stop yapping and start eating. You can slurp it with a spoon or gulp it right out of the bowl," she said. "We ain't much for table manners around here."

"Yeah. I figured manners left the room when you poured poison in the pot."

"Go on. Eat up," Polly said.

"Is the stew at least any good?" Sam asked, stalling.

"I made it from scratch," Polly answered. "What do you think?"

Sam looked at the bowl and shook his head. "No offense. I'm sure it's delicious. But, like I said, I'm really not that hungry."

"I'll force-feed it to you if I have to," Polly said. "I'm doing you the courtesy of letting you die with a little dignity."

Sam looked at the sheriff, noticing that guilt again.

"You know, people know I'm here. And I've got friends in a lot higher places than Amy did," he said. "Will you be ready when teams of state investigators start swarming this place?"

The sheriff swallowed hard and looked at Polly, but her stone-cold glare put more fear in him than a thousand law enforcement officers. Sam, realizing his options were running out, picked up the spoon and stirred it around in the bowl.

"What the hell, might as well jump in the deep end."

He picked up the bowl and brought it to his lips. Then, right before he took a gulp, he let out an explosive sneeze, dropping the bowl to the floor and splattering stew everywhere.

"Oh, excuse me. I'm so sorry."

Polly looked down at the mess.

"What the hell tarnation is wrong with you?" she yelled.

"Sorry. That garlic smell got to me," Sam said. "I'll clean it up."

"You don't move," Polly said. "I got a lot more where that came from. But this time, I'll feed you myself."

Sam turned to the sheriff. "When those state investigators figure out what's going on – and they will – you think you'll get charged with aiding and abetting, or as a full accomplice? I'd put my money on second degree murder, for sure."

The sheriff's gaze ping-ponged between Polly and Sam.

"Miss Polly, maybe we need to re-think this," he muttered.

"Oh, don't you go soft on me now," Polly said. "He's bluffing."

"Check my phone," Sam said. "Check the texts. You can see the pictures I sent to my wife."

Sam offered his phone to the sheriff, who yanked it out of his hands and started scrolling.

"He ain't bluffing."

"You're already going down," Sam said softly to the sheriff. "How far down is up to what you do right now."

Polly approached with a fresh bowl, but the sheriff stood abruptly. "Miss Polly, it's time to stop all this."

"Sit down," she growled.

The sheriff grabbed the bowl from her. "No. This has gone far enough. Turning a blind eye was one thing, but you've pulled me in too deep. I'm done."

Polly stared at him, aghast, as he poured the stew into the sink.

"I can't believe my own brother-in-law would betray me like this. Randall would be ashamed."

"You leave my brother out of this," the sheriff said.

"Fine," Polly snarled.

She snatched the sheriff's gun that he had left on the table, and pointed it back and forth between the two men. "As always, I gotta do everything myself."

"Polly, put the gun down," the sheriff said.

She cocked the hammer. "You brought this on yourself, Sebastian."

Before she could pull the trigger, another voice shattered the room.

"Freeze!"

Constable Clyde's mumbled voice cracked through

the air like a whip. He stood on the other side of the kitchen – bruised, battered, barely upright, and aiming his gun at Polly with his one good arm.

Sam didn't wait. He lunged at Polly, tackling her to the floor. The sheriff stepped toward them, but Clyde turned his gun on him.

"Sit. Down. Now."

51

As soon as Polly had left Clyde's hospital room, he had texted a warning to Sam then pulled himself out of bed, forced himself into his bloody clothes, and slumped out of the hospital.

With his SUV either still at Diamond's or impounded – and his badge and gun inside of it – he flagged down a nurse he knew and, trying to hide his wooziness, begged to borrow her car for police business. Fortunately, she was thrilled to be a part of something that seemed like exciting police business and agreed without question. Clyde drove carefully, forcing his focus to stay in his lane as he made a quick stop at his house for his spare gun before racing to Polly's house.

Sam had told Clyde the full plan so he knew Carla

was at the County Records department with Walter. He dialed the office and told Carla to call the Texas Rangers. He knew they would ignore his call, but were likely to take the request from a respected medical examiner. Still, he couldn't be sure and didn't know how long it would take for them to respond.

It took him a few minutes but he finally swerved his way to Polly's house. Seeing no other vehicles there, Clyde parked by the road. Running on adrenaline but still fighting the painkillers running through him, he stumbled his way up to the house and slipped inside, limping to the kitchen just in time.

After wrestling the sheriff's gun from Polly, Sam picked her up off the floor and set her in the chair opposite the sheriff.

"Sam, can you take this?" Clyde asked weakly as he started to slide down the wall.

Sam took his gun from him and held it on his former captors while Clyde leaned against the wall beside him.

"You okay?" Sam asked.

"Not even a little bit," Clyde mumbled.

Sam grabbed his phone off the table to call for back-up, but State Troopers stormed through the door before he could dial. He quickly and calmly set the guns on the floor and raised both hands immediately to show he wasn't a threat. Clyde mustered up just enough strength to point them toward Polly and the sheriff.

As two Rangers escorted the pair outside, Carla arrived – her car barely coming to a stop before she leapt out of it. She sprinted to Sam and threw her arms around him. As they kissed, she caught a strong whiff of garlic and chemicals.

"Why do you smell like pesticide and beef stew?" she asked.

"Long story short, Miss Polly made me a homemade meal to die for. She's got lots more in the kitchen. Along with gallons of the pesticide."

Carla nodded, immediately putting all the pieces together. She grabbed another one of the Rangers by the arm.

"She was poisoning people with organophosphate insecticide. It's highly toxic if ingested in large amounts. That's how she tried to murder my husband and most likely the way she killed Amy Booker."

"My guess is she was also dosing others slowly over time," Sam added.

Carla nodded. "Amy was starting to make the connection. She knew something suspicious was going on, but just hadn't connected all the dots yet. But if we exhume a few bodies, I'm pretty sure we can prove it. And now that we know what we're looking for, I can test Amy's blood for the right poison, too."

Polly twisted around as they loaded her into the Rangers' vehicle "You can't prove I did any of it."

Across the driveway, the sheriff stood handcuffed beside a different Ranger vehicle, his shoulders collapsed under the weight of shame.

"It's true," Sheriff Wheeler said quietly. "All of it. She was poisoning people to get their land and she poisoned Amy when she started asking questions."

He swallowed hard and lifted his head. "Then you started sniffing around, so I staged her body to look like a hanging. Just like you said."

Then his face broke.

"I'm also the one that killed Skeeter Wells," His voice cracked as he continued. "He saw me taking Amy's body to his old house. I did it. I killed him. She asked me to. Told me to frame him for Amy's death while I was at it."

"He's lying!" Polly yelled.

A piercing ambulance siren cut through the air.

"I called paramedics, too," Carla said. "In case we were too late."

"Good. He's gonna need it," Sam said, motioning back toward the house as a Texas Ranger helped Clyde hobble out.

"Take note, boys," Sam said to the Rangers. "This is what a real hero looks like."

The EMTs rushed toward Clyde with a gurney and helped him onto it. As they wheeled him past Sam, Clyde looked up proudly. "I told you we'd get 'em."

Sam smiled back. "That you did."

52

———

A COUPLE OF MONTHS LATER, things had finally settled into something resembling normal in Burdett County. Several of the bodies whose names had been circled on Polly's list had been exhumed, each showing enough traces of poison to build a case. High levels of organophosphate toxins were also found in Amy's body, allowing R.J. to amend the official cause of death to "Respiratory failure due to acute organophosphate toxicity" with the manner of death listed as "Homicide."

With the poison identified, many of the residents, like Lila Mae, were able to get the proper treatment for their illnesses and they soon were able to recover fully.

The case went to trial about six months later. The sheriff, overcome with guilt and remorse, cooperated fully with authorities, confessing to every last bit of his part in Miss Polly's scheme. While he had worked out an immunity deal for his complicity in the poisonings, he was still handed a life sentence for Skeeter's murder.

Polly stubbornly insisted on her innocence, claiming all she ever wanted to do was help her community. Plenty of folks believed her, too. They just wanted to hold on to the idea that she'd been the town's guardian angel, despite the overwhelming evidence against that notion. It goes against most people's nature to believe a person could have both halo and horns. Eventually, however, Polly Wheeler was charged with ten counts of second-degree murder and one count of first-degree murder for Amy's death, receiving a life sentence plus eighty years. All the land she'd accumulated was returned to surviving family members. The county took over any unclaimed property and auctioned it back to the community.

Miss Polly being Miss Polly, it didn't take long before she had not only adjusted to prison life but was pretty much running the show.

With the sheriff out of the picture, Constable Clyde stepped up as the county's main law enforcement. While he had garnered a newfound respect among many townspeople, a handful still bristled over his role in bringing down their beloved Miss Polly. Still, he found enough support to run for County Sheriff in an uncontested election. Even though he didn't need it, he insisted on putting up a billboard on the main road near Gus Booker's house – a giant photo of Clyde kneeling next to Boone, his newly rescued hound The billboard smiled down at Gus every time he drove past it.

Speaking of Gus, after finding the notes in his bedroom, he had been convinced Skeeter had killed Amy and swore to avenge her death. Fortunately, like most things Gus set out to do, his vengeance petered out in less than twenty-four hours when he was distracted by the allure of a cold beer. And Mandy.

After his fight with Clyde, he had taken the path of least resistance right into Mandy's arms. The couple tied the knot not long after Amy was buried, but it became the shortest marriage on public record in Burdett County when Mandy left Gus for the man who had issued their wedding license: Walter Puckett.

As for Sam and Carla, they regularly visited Burdett County – partly for court hearings and testimony, but also to check in on Clyde and some of their other new friends, including R.J. Sanders, who had let go of his resentment toward Carla and seemed re-energized with a fresh love for his job. Of course, it didn't hurt that Carla had kept her promise to let him take credit as the tenacious coroner who wouldn't give up until he uncovered the truth. To his credit, he had offered to share the spotlight, but Carla wasn't interested. Justice was her trophy. Besides, it would just have meant more court depositions.

Sam, on the other hand, was not nearly as humble. After all, the more credit he got, the more potential clients he could attract. With the help of Walter, he helped Toby and Lila Mae form a small homeowners association to protect Cypress Meadows from future predators. He even spearheaded an investigation, at no cost, into Southern Sun Properties to determine whether or not they were complicit in Polly's land grab. They settled out of court – giving the association ample funds to not only make some much-needed repairs to some of the homes but also build a community pool.

A few months later, Sun Properties would announce they'd be breaking ground on the luxury hotel they had planned... on property they had recently acquired from Polly Wheeler. Knowing she'd never be returning to her home, and having no children, Miss Polly had agreed to sell her property below market value to the real estate firm, handing every penny to the county in a last-ditch attempt to repair her legacy. The new property would bring new jobs and a flood of money into the county.

It also turns out Amy had a generous life insurance policy and had named Judy as the sole beneficiary. Partly out of guilt for being strong-armed by the sheriff but mainly out of gratitude, Judy had insisted on giving a portion of the hefty payout to Sam. He had used the money to buy a 16-foot fishing boat, currently parked proudly in his his driveway as he washed it for the tenth time in a week.

"There you are," Carla said. "I'm beginning to get jealous of this thing."

Sam grinned, releasing the spray gun on the end of the hose. "I will happily give you a bath next if you want."

Carla slipped her arms around his waist. "I bet you would."

"I'm taking her out Saturday morning. You wanna come with me?"

"You leave much too early in the morning for me," Carla said. "I'll join you for a sunset cruise any day, though."

Sam kissed her. "That is a date I promise to keep."

He set down the hose and the couple walked back to the house, passing the freshly painted name on the boat's stern:

SKEETER'S DREAMS

Thank you for reading

LEAVE DEAD ENOUGH ALONE

If you enjoyed it, be sure to leave a review wherever you
bought your copy.

<u>**MORE SAM LAWSON MYSTERY SERIES**</u>

COMBUSTIBLE (Book 1)

BENEATH THE SURFACE (Book 2)

DARK HARBOR (Book 3)

DEADLY REPUTATION (Book 4)

DEATH ON LOCATION (Book 5)

BEFORE HER LAST BREATH (Book 6)

MURDER IN SPA CITY (Book 7)

<u>**GET A FREE COPY OF *BOUND BY MURDER***</u>

To download a free copy, scan the code or visit david

kwilsonauthor.com

ACKNOWLEDGMENTS

Thank you as always to my team of first readers: Amy Franklin, Shelley Upchurch, Lorraine Evanoff, Barbara Fournier, Yvonne Pelletier, James Hewitson and, of course, the Texas Tornadoes: Regina Riddle and Rena Grubbs. You all never fail to elevate my work and I'm so grateful for you all.

Special thanks also goes out to cover designer JT Lindroos, who took over in a pinch and hit it out of the park.

A big heap of gratitude gravy also goes out to the ever-growing community of authors who have let me be a part of their world. I'm blessed to know each of you. And it would be neglectful – and possibly even dangerous – to not thank my friends and family who continue to support me.

Finally, thanks to all of the readers who have waited almost two years for a new Sam adventure. Your kind words and encouragement mean more to me than you know and are what keep me going..

ABOUT THE AUTHOR

David K. Wilson grew up in East Texas, surrounded by enough colorful characters to fill the pages of hundreds of books. In addition to being the author of the popular Sam Lawson Mystery series and the highly lauded crime comedy, *Red Dirt Blues*, and award-winning *The Girl in the Whispers*. David is also a seasoned ghostwriter and screenwriter. He currently lives in upstate New York.

Sign up to receive updates, promos and more at davidkwilsonauthor.com.

instagram.com/davidkwilsonauthor

facebook.com/davidkwilsonauthor

tiktok.com/@davidkwilsonauthor

goodreads.com/davidkwilson